Labrador Days

NORTHWARD HO!

Labrador Days

TALES OF THE SEA TOILERS

By

Wilfred Thomason Grenfell
M. D. (OXON.), C. M. G.

Fredonia Books
Amsterdam, The Netherlands

Labrador Days:
Tales of the Sea Toilers

by
Wilfred Thomason Grenfell

ISBN: 1-58963-858-1

Reprinted from the 1919 edition

Fredonia Books
Amsterdam, The Netherlands
http://www.fredoniabooks.com

Contents

Labrador Days

THERE'S TROUBLE ON THE SEA

THE ice in the big bay had broken up suddenly
that year in the latter part of March before a
tremendous ocean swell heaving in beneath it.
The piles of firewood and the loads of timber
for the summer fishing-rooms on all the outer
islands were left standing on the landwash.
The dog-teams usually haul all this out at a
stretch gallop over the glare ice which overlies
in April the snow-covered surface of winter.
For weeks, heavy pack ice, driven to and fro
with the tides, but ever held in the bay with
the onshore winds, had prevented the small
boats' freighting more than their families and
the merest necessities to the summer stations.

So it came to pass that long after the usual
time, indeed after the incoming shoals of fish
were surely expected, John Mitchell's firewood
still lay on the bank, some twenty miles up

1

the bay. When at last a spell of warm and off-shore winds had driven the ice mostly clear, John announced to his eager lads that "come Monday, if the wind held westerly," he would go up the bay for a load. What a clamour ensued, for every one wanted to be one of the crew to go to the winter home. The lads, like ducklings, "fair loved the water"; and though John needed Jim, and was quite glad to have Tom, now of the important age of fourteen years, he did his best, well seconded by the wise old grandmother, to persuade Neddie, aged twelve, and Willie, aged ten, to stay behind.

"You be too small, Ned, yet awhile. Next year perhaps father will take you," was the old lady's first argument. "'T will be cold in t' boat, boy, and you'll perish altogether."

"Father'll look after me, Grannie, and I'll wrap up ever so warm. Do let me go. There's a dear grannie."

The curly-haired, rosy-cheeked lads were so insistent and so winsome that the old lady confessed to me afterwards, "They somehow got

There's Trouble on the Sea

round my heart as they mostly does, and I let 'em go, though sore against my mind, Doctor."

Of course, Willie had to go if Neddie went, for "they'd be company while t' men worked, and he could carry small things as well as t' rest. He did so want to go."

When at length Monday came, and a bright sun shone over a placid sea, the grandmother's last excuse to keep them at home was lost. Her consent was finally secured, and, before a light, fair wind the women watched, not without anxiety, so many of those whom they held dearer than life itself sail "out into the deep."

Progress was slow, for the wind fell away almost altogether as the morning passed, but the glorious warmth and exuberance of life made the time seem as nothing. The picnic in the big trap boat was as good as a prince's banquet. For the fun of "boiling t' kettle yourself," and an appetite bred of a day on the water, made the art of French cooks and the stimulus of patent relishes pale into insignificance. During the afternoon they "had a spurt singing," and as the words of hymns were the only ones they knew, the old favourites were sung and resung. The little lads especially led the programme; and the others remembered Willie singing for them, as a solo, a childish favourite called "Bring Them In."

It was just about seven o'clock in the evening. The boat was well out in the bay, between three and four miles from land, when John noticed a fresh "cat's-paw" of wind, just touching the water here and there. There was scarcely a cloud in the sky, and nothing whatever to suggest a squall. But as he looked again, a suspicious wisp of white water lifted suddenly from the surface a few yards to windward. Like a flash he remembered that the boat had no ballast in her, and was running with her sheets made fast. Instinctively he leaned forward to let go the foresail, but at the same moment the squall struck the boat like the hammer of Thor. Relieved of the fore canvas, the trap should have come to the wind in an instant. Instead, leaning over heavily with the immense pressure, she staggered and reeled

There's Trouble on the Sea

as if some unseen enemy had gripped her. Scarcely perceptibly she gave ground, and a lifetime seemed to elapse to John's horror-stricken mind as she fell slowly over, as if fighting for every inch, and conscious of her terrible responsibilities for the issues at stake.

At last, in spite of her stout resistance, and before John could climb aft and get at the main sheet, or do anything to relieve the boat, her stern was driven right under water by the sheer pressure of the storm. Slowly she turned over, leaving all of her occupants struggling in the icy water, for there were many pieces of ice still "knocking around."

The slow rate at which the boat had gone over was one point in their favour, however, for it enabled even the little lads to get clear of the gunwale; and by the help of John and Jim all five were soon huddled on the upturned keel of the boat. The boys being all safe for the moment, John rubbed his eyes, and, raising himself as high as he could, viewed the situation. Alas! the squall had come to stay. Everywhere now the placid surface of the sea was ruffled and angry. The rising, flaky clouds convinced him even in that instantaneous glance that the brewing storm offered them little chance for their lives.

Far away to leeward, not less than four miles distant, the loom of the land was only just visible. Well he realized that it would be many long hours before the boat, with her masts and sails still fast in, could drive near enough to enable them to make a landing. For, like most fishermen in these icy waters, none of them knew how to swim. Moreover, he soon found that the anchor, fast to the warp, had fallen out, and would certainly sooner or later touch bottom — thus robbing them of their one and only chance of escape by preventing the boat from drifting into shallow water.

So cold was it already that it appeared as if a few moments at most must chill the life out of at least the younger children.

"Hold Willie on, Ned, and ask God to bring us all safe home," said John. He told me that he felt somehow as if their prayers were more likely to be heard than his own. He then

crawled forward, having made up his mind to
try and cut the anchor free, and to get the rope
to tie round the boat and hold on the children.
His determination was fortified by his anxiety;
but it was a forlorn hope, for it meant lowering
himself right into the water, and he knew well
enough that he could not swim a yard. Then it
was done, and he was once more clinging to
the keel with the rope in his hand. It was not
difficult to get a bight round the boat, and
soon he had the children firmly lashed on and
the boat was again making fair progress before
the wind to the opposite shore.

Hours seemed to go by. The children were
sleepy. Apparently they no longer felt the
cold, and the average man might have thought
that it was a miracle on their behalf, for God
knows they had prayed hard enough for one.
But John recognized only too well that it was
that merciful harbinger of the last long sleep,
which had overtaken more than one of his best
friends, when adrift in the storms of winter.
And still the age-long journey dragged hopelessly on.

Labrador Days

At last the awful suspense, a thousand times more cruel for their being unable to do anything, was broken by even the welcome incident of a new danger. Breakers were visible in the direct course of their drift. "Maybe she'll turn over, Jim," whispered the skipper. "I reckon we must loose t' children for fear she does." This being effected as promptly as their condition allowed, Tom was told off to do nothing but watch them and keep them safe. For already the men had planned, if the slightest chance offered, to try and get the masts out while she lay on her beam-ends.

The breakers? Well, they knew they were only of small extent. There was a pinnacle of rock and a single sea might possibly carry them over it; but the peril of being washed off was none the less. Now they could see the huge rise of the combing sea with its frowning black top rushing at the shoal, and smashing into an avalanche of snowy foam. They could hear the dull roar of the sea, and its mighty thunder, as it curled over and fell furiously upon itself, for want of other prey.

There's Trouble on the Sea

"Good-bye, Jim," whispered the skipper. "The children is all right either way, but one of us may come through. Tell 'em home it was all right if I goes."

Almost as he stopped speaking, the rising swell caught the craft, and threw her once more on her beam-ends. As for a moment she lay on her side, the men attempted to free the masts, but could do nothing, for the boat almost immediately again fell over, bottom up. But a second comber, lifting her with redoubled violence, threw them all clear of the boat, turned her momentarily right way up, and then breaking into the masts and sails, tipped her for the third time upside down, flinging her at the same instant in mad fury clear of the angry water. So violent had been the blow which had thrown them clear, that they must inevitably all have perished, had not the last effort of the breakers actually hurled the boat again almost on the top of them. Clutching as at a straw, the two men caught the loops of the rope which they had wound round their craft, but they could see nothing of the other three. Suddenly, from almost directly under the boat, Tom's head appeared within reach. Grabbing him, they tried to drag him up on to the keel. Rolling in the wake of the breakers which still followed them with vicious pertinacity, they twice lost their hold of the boy, their now numbed limbs scarcely giving them strength to grasp anything. It seemed of little account at the time either way. But their third attempt was successful, and they got the lad once more on to the bottom of the boat.

Of the children they saw no more. Only when Tom had revived somewhat could he explain that the capsizing boat had caught them all three under it as in a trap, that he had succeeded, still clinging to Willie, to get him from under it, and that he was still holding his brother when he first came to the surface. After that he did not remember anything till they were calling to him on the boat's bottom. The men were sure that it was so — that because he had been true to the last to his trust, he had been such a deadweight the first two times he came to the surface.

There's Trouble on the Sea

And now began again the cruel, wearisome, endless drift of the water-logged boat toward the still distant shore, lightened but little by the loss of the loved children. There was no longer any doubt left in their minds; unless something could be done, none of them would possibly live to tell the tale. It was the still active mind and indomitable courage of the skipper which found the solution. Crawling close to Jim, he said: "There's only one chance. We must turn her over, and get in her, or perish. I'm going to try and loose t' masts."

Swinging himself once more into the bitter-cold water, he succeeded in finding the slight ropes which formed the stays, and though it is almost incredible, he actually managed to cut and free them all, before Jim hauled him back, more dead than alive, on to the boat's bottom. At all hazards they must right the boat and climb into her. Their plans were soon made. Tom, placed between the two men, was to do exactly as they did. Stretching themselves out, and holding the keel rope in their hands, they

all threw themselves over on one side, lying as
nearly as possible at full length. The boat responded instantly, and their only fear was
that, as she had done before, she might again
go right over on them. But there were no masts
now to hold the wind, so she stood up on her
beam-ends. As the water took the weights of
the men, it was all they could do to get her
over. Moreover, the task was rendered doubly
difficult and perilous by their exhaustion and
inability to swim when the keel to which they
were holding went under water. But their agil-
ity and self-reliance, evolved from a life next
to Nature, stood them in good stead, and soon
all three were actually standing inside the
water-logged boat. The oars, lashed under the
seats, were still in her, and, though almost up
to their waists in water, they began sculling
and rowing as hard as their strength and the
dangerous roll of the sunken boat would per-
mit.

Slowly the surf on the sandy beach drew
near, and now, keeping her head before the
breeze, they rolled along shorewards. Again,

There's Trouble on the Sea

however, it became apparent that a new departure must be made. For a heavy surf was breaking on the shore which they were approaching, that ran off shallow for half a mile. There was not water enough to let the boat approach the land, and they realized that they had not sufficient strength left to walk through the breakers. Yet struggle as they would, the best they could do was to keep the boat very slightly across the wind.

John maintains now that it was the direct intervention of Providence which spared them just when once more all hope seemed over. They suddenly noticed that while still forging shorewards they were also drifting rapidly into the bay. It was the first uprush of the strong rising tide, and they might yet be carried to a deep-water landing. The play of hope and fear made the remaining hours an agony of suspense. What would be the end of it all seemed a mere gamble. Every mark on the approaching shore was now familiar to them. It had become, they knew well enough, a question of life or death where the drifting boat would touch the strand. Now it seemed impossible that she should clear the shallow surf, whose hungry roar sounded a death-knell to any one handed to its tender mercies. Now it seemed certain that she would be carried up the bay without touching land at all. Hope rose as a little later it became obvious that she would clear the sands.

Now the rocky headland, round which their winter house stood, was coming rapidly into view. As the mouth of the bay narrowed, the pace of the current increased, and for a time they seemed to be hopelessly rushing past their one hope of landing. The excitement and the exertion of putting might and main into the oars had made them almost forget the wet and cold and darkness, now only relieved by the last afterglow of the setting sun. But it all appeared of no avail; they were still some hundred yards off as they passed the point. It might as well have been some hundred miles, for they drifted helplessly into the bay, which was widening out again.

Despair, however, still failed to grip them,

There's Trouble on the Sea

and apparently hopelessly they kept toiling on at the sweeps. Once more a miracle happened, and they were really apparently approaching the point a second time. The very violence of the tide had actually saved them, creating as it did a strong eddy, which with the little aid from the oars, bore them now steadily toward the land. Nearer and nearer they came. They were half a mile inside the head. Only a few boat-lengths now separated them from the beach. Would they be able to get ashore!

Strange as it sounds, any and all speculations they might have with regard to where the boat would strike bottom were to be disappointed. Her keel never touched bottom at all. It was her gunwale which first bumped into the steep rocks — and that at a point only a few yards from their winter house.

Even now their troubles were not over. Only the skipper could stand erect. Tom, dragged out by the others, lay an inert mass on the soft bed of crisp creeping plants which cover the bank. Jim was able to totter a few

15

yards, fell, and finally crawled part of the way to the house door. But the skipper, in spite of swollen and blackened legs, held out not only to get a fire lit, but to bring in the other two, and finally wean back their frozen limbs to life.

It took two days to regain strength enough to haul up the boat and refit her; and then the sorrowful little company proceeded on their homeward journey. It was a sad home-coming after the brave start they had made. It was a terrible message which they had to carry to the anxious hearts awaiting them. For nothing in heaven or earth can replace the loss of loved ones suddenly taken from us.

"I've been cruising in boats five and forty years," said John. "I were out two days and a night with t' Bonnie Lass when she were lost on t' Bristle Rocks, and us brought in only two of her crew alive. And I was out on t' ice in t' blizzard when Jim Warren drove off, and us brought he back dead to his wife next day. But this was the worst of all. As us passed t' rocky shoal, it seemed only a few minutes since us capsized on it; and I knowed Ned and Willie

must be right alongside. As us passed Snarly
Bight, out of which t' puff came, us thought of
t' boys singing their little songs, and know'd
that they should be with us now; and when t'
Lone Point loomed up, round which youse turn
to make our harbour, us all sort of wished one
more puff would come along and finish t' job
properly. For it would n't have been hard to
join t' children again, but to face t' women
without 'em seemed more 'n us could do.

"How to break the news us had talked a
dozen times, but never got no nearer what to
say. As us ran in at last for t' stage, us could see
that Mother had hoisted t' flag t' Company
gived we t' year us bought furs for they, and
that Grannie was out waiting for us on t' landwash.

"All I remembers was that scarce a word
was spoke. They know'd it. I believe they
know'd it before they seed t' boat. If only
them had cried I 'd have been able to say something. But ne'er a word was spoke. So I says,
'Jim, go up and pull t' flag down quick. Us has
no right to having t' flags flying for we.'

Labrador Days

"Then Grannie, she gets her voice, and she says, 'No, Jimmie, don't you do it. It be just right as it is. For 't is for Neddie's and Willie's home-coming it be flying.'"

NANCY

WE had just reached hospital from a long trip "on dogs." My driver was slipping the harnesses off the animals and giving them the customary friendly cuff and words of praise. Among the crowd which always gathered to greet us, one friend, after giving us the usual welcome of "What cheer, Doctor?" noticed apparently that I had a new winter *compagnon de voyage*.

"Joe's not with you, Doctor? Gone sawing t' winter, I hear. T' boys say he's got a fine bulk of timber cut already."

"Working for the lumber camp, I suppose, Uncle Abe," I replied.

"Not a bit of it," he chuckled. "'T is sawing for hisself he's gone."

"Eh? Wants lumber, does he? Going to build a larger fishing boat?"

"Youse can call it that if you likes, Doctor, for 't will be a fine fish he lands into it. But I reckon 't is more of a dock he'll need." And the rest joined in hearty laughter at the sally.

"'T is a full-rigged schooner he be going to moor there, with bunting enough to burn, and as saucy as a cyclone," chimed in another, while a third 'lowed, "'T is a great girl he's after, if he gets her, anyhow."

"Nancy's the pluckiest little girl for many a mile along this coast or she would n't be what she is, and her family so poor."

A week or so later I fell in with half a dozen boisterous lads driving their sledges home laden with new wood. It proclaimed to the harbour that the rumour of Joe's big bulk of timber being ready so early had not been exaggerated. It was only then that I learned that he had in addition quickly got his floors down before the ground froze, so that he might finish building before the winter set in.

Many hands make light work and every one was Joe's friend, so by the end of December the new house had not only been sheathed in, but roofed and floored, ready for occupation.

In our scattered communities, isolated not

only from one another, but also largely from the world outside, the simple incidents of everyday life afford just as much interest as the more artificial attractions of civilization. Every one on our coast in winter has to have a dog team, no matter how poor he is, in order to haul home his firewood. In summer there is no time and there are no roads, while in winter the snow makes the whole land one broad highway. There is no better fun than a "randy" over the snow on a light komatik. At this time even our older people go on "joy rides," visiting along the coast. Many a moonlight night, after the day's work is over, when the reflection from the snow makes it almost as light as day, an unexpected but welcome visitor comes knocking at one's door, asking for a shake-down just for the night.

Thus Joe's secret was soon common property. His own enthusiasm, however, engendered a reflection of itself in other people, and almost before he had the cottage sheathed inside, and really "ready for launching," from here and there every one had come in, bringing

at any rate the necessities to make it possible
to put out to sea on the new voyage. Accordingly I was not surprised one evening a little
later when a low knock at my door, followed
by a summons to come in, revealed Joe standing somewhat sheepishly, cap in hand, in the
entrance. Once the subject was broached, however, the matter was soon arranged, Joe having
a direct way about him which ignored difficulties, and I, being a Justice of the Peace, was
soon pledged to act as parson at the function.

Everything went well. We struck glorious
weather for the day of the wedding. Little dep-
utations streamed in from other villages; gay
flags and banners, though some of fearsome
home-devised patterns, made a brave contrast
to the white mantle of snow; while we supple-
mented the usual salvo of guns from portentous and historic fowling-pieces with a halo of
distress rockets, which we burned from our
hospital boat, which was lying frozen in our
harbour.

The excitement of the affair, like all other
things human, soon passed away, and the ordi-

nary routine of the wood-path, the fur-path, and seal-hunting, the saw-pit, the net-loft, and boat-building, turned our attention to our own affairs once more. The new venture was soon an old one, only we were glad to see, as we passed along the road, a fresh column of blue smoke rising, and speaking of another centre of life and activity in our village.

Once more, as the sun crept north of the line, the ice bonds of our harbour began to melt. Once more the mighty ocean outside, freed from the restraint of the Arctic floe, generously sent surging into the landwash the very power we needed, and on which we depend, to break up and carry out the heavy ice accumulation of the winter, which must otherwise bar us altogether from the prosecution of our calling.

My own vessel had been scraped and repainted. Her spars bright with new varnish, her funnel gay with our blue bunting flag contrasting with the yellow, she had come to the wharf for the last time before leaving for the long summer cruise among the Labrador fishing fleet. Indeed, I was just working over the ship's course in my chart-room, when once more Joe, cap in hand, stood in the doorway — evidently with something very much on his mind.

"What is it, Joe? Come in and shut the door and sit down. You are only just in time, for I was going to ring for steam as you came along."

"Well, Doctor," he said, "'t is this way. I 's only got hook and line to fish with as you knows; and that don't give a fellow a chance of putting anything by, no matter how well he does. There's no knowing now but what I may need more still. It is n't like when a man was alone in the world. I was aboard Captain Jackson of the Water Lily, what come in last night, and he says that he 'd take me to the Labrador fishing, and give me a share in his cod trap, being as he is short of a hand. Well, 't is a fine chance, Doctor. But Nancy won't hear of my going without her going too. She says that she is well able to do it, and well acquainted with schooners — and that's true, as you knows; but I'm afraid to take her as she is. Still, 't is a good chance, and I did n't like to let it go, so I just come to ask what your mind is about it."

I had seen Nancy on my farewell round of the cottages, and although I should have preferred almost any other occupation for her, yet, taking into consideration the habits and customs of the people, and that to her the venture was in no way a new one, I advised him to accept the skipper's offer, and take Nancy along with him, if they could get decent accommodation. I received his assurance that he would keep a lookout for the hospital boat. With most sincere protestations of gratitude he bade me farewell, and when a few minutes later we steamed past his little house on our way out to sea, he was all ready with his long gun to fire us good-bye salutes, which we answered and re-answered with our steam whistle.

All summer long we were cruising off the northern Labrador coast, now running into the fjords to visit the scattered settlers, now on the outside among the many fishing craft which were plying their calling on the banks that fringe the islands and outermost points of land.

Labrador Days

Fishermen from hundreds of vessels visited us for sickness, for books, for a thousand different reasons; but never a sight of the Water Lily did we see, and never a word did we hear of either Joe or Nancy the whole season through. True, in the number of other claims on our attention, it was not often that their fortunes came to one's mind. But now and again we asked about the schooner, and always got the same negative reply, "Reckon she've got a load and gone south." This was a view which we were only too glad to adopt, as it meant the best possible luck for our friends.

Now November had come round once more. The main fleet of vessels had long ago passed south. It was so long since we had seen even one of the belated craft which "bring up the heel of the Labrador" that we had closed up the summer stations, and were paying our last visits to our colleagues at the southern hospital, who were to remain through the winter.

It was therefore no small surprise when Jake Low, from the village, who had been up spying from the lookout on the hill, came into the hospital and announced that a large schooner with a flag flying in her rigging was beating up to the harbour mouth from sea. "She's making good ground and is well fished," he added. "What's more, I guess from t' course she's shaping they know the way in all right. So it must be a doctor they wants, and not a pilot at this time of year."

The news proved interesting enough to lure us up to the hilltop with the telescope, where in a short while we were enjoying the wonderful spectacle of watching a crew of the vikings of our day force their way through a winding narrow passage in a large vessel against a heavy winter head wind.

The tide, too, was running out against her, and now and then a flaw of wind or a back eddy, caused by the cliffs on either side, would upset the helmsman's calculations. Yet with superb coolness he would drive her, till to us watchers, lying stretched out on the ground overhead, it seemed that her forefoot must surely be over the submerged cliff-side. Certainly the white surf from the rocks washed her cutwater before the skipper who was "scunning" or directing, perched on the fore crosstree, would sing out the "Ready about. Lee, oh!" for which the men at the sheets and bowlines were keenly waiting.

A single slip, and she would have cracked like a nutshell against those adamantine walls. But to get into the harbour it was the only way, and as the skipper said afterwards, when I remonstrated on his apparent foolhardiness, "Needs must, when the devil drives."

"There's a big crowd of men on deck, Doctor," said my companion. "Reckon she's been delayed with her freighters, and that there's a load of women and children in t' hold on t' fish."

I had been so absorbed in watching his seamanship, that I had not been thinking about the stranger. Jake's remark changed the current of my thoughts; and soon the vessel's lines seemed to assume a familiar shape, and I began to realize that I must have seen her before. Then suddenly it flashed upon me — the Water Lily, of course.

Nancy

Yes, it was the Water Lily. Then Joe was on board, and the flag was because Nancy was in trouble. The reasoning was intuitive rather than didactic; but the conviction was so forcible that I instinctively rose to return to the hospital for the black bag that is my *fidus Achates* on every emergency call.

"You is n't going till she rounds t' point of t' Chain Rocks, is you, Doctor? It's all she'll do with the wind and tide against her — if she does it. I minds more than one good vessel that's left her bones on them reefs."

"As well stay, I suppose, Jake, for I'll be in time if I do. My! look at that!" I could not help shouting, as a flaw of wind struck the schooner right ahead as she was actually in stays, and it seemed she must either fall in sideways or drive stern foremost on the cliffs. But almost as quick as the eddy, the staysail and jib were let run and off her, and her main boom was pushed by a whole gang of men away out over the rail, so that by altering the points of pressure the good ship went safely round on her heel, and before we had time to discuss

it, her head sails were up again, and she was
racing on her last tack to enable her to claw
through the narrow channel between the Chain
Rocks and the Cannons, which form the last
breakwater for the harbour.

"I think she'll do it, Jake!"

"If she once gets in t' narrows and can't
fetch t' point, it's all up with her. I 'lows 't is
time to get them women out of t' hold, anyhow," he replied laconically, his eyes riveted
all the while on the scene below. "There's a
crowd standing by t' boat, I sees, and them's
putting a line in her," he added a minute or
two later, during which time excitement had
prevented either of us from speaking. "Us'll
know in a second one way or t' other."

The crisis had soon arrived. The schooner
had once more reached across the harbour
channel, and was for the last time "in stays."
A decision had to be arrived at instantly, and
on it, and on the handling of the vessel, de-
pended her fate.

"He's game, sure enough, whoever he is.
He's going for it hit or miss." And there was a

touch of excitement evidenced even in Jake's undemonstrative exterior.

We could now plainly see the master. He was standing on the cross-tree, whence he could tell, by looking into the water, almost to an inch how far it was possible to go before turning.

"She'll do it, Jake, she'll do it. See, she's heading for the middle of the run."

"She will if she does, and that's all, Doctor. She's falling off all t' while."

It was only too true. The vessel could no longer head for the point. Her sails were aback, shaking in the wind, and she now heading straight for the rock itself. Surely she must at once try to come up in the wind, stop her way, drop her sails, if possible throw out the boat, and head for the open before she should strike on one side or the other of the run.

But no, we could hear the stentorian tones of the skipper on the cross-trees shouting that which to any but an experienced sailor must have seemed certain suicide. "Keep her away! Keep her — full! Don't starve her! Give her way! Up topsail!" — the latter having been let down to allow the vessel to lie closer hauled to the wind. "Stand by to douse the head sails! Stand by the topsail!" we heard him shout. "Stand by to shoot her into the wind!" — and then at last, just as the crash seemed inevitable, "Hard down! Shoot her up! Down sails!"

We up above, with our hearts in our mouths, saw the plucky little vessel shoot true as a die up for the point. It was her only chance. I am sure that I could have heard my own heart beating as I saw her rise on the swell that ran up on the point, and it seemed to me she stopped and hung there. But before I could be certain whether she was ashore or not, another flood of the swell had rushed over the point, and she was fairly swirled around and dropped down into the safety of the harbour.

"It's time to be going, Doctor," Jake remarked as he rose from the ground. "But I 'low t' point won't want painting t' winter," he added, with a twinkle in his eye. "Howsomever, he's a good one, he is, wherever he be from, and I don't care who says 't ain't so" — high praise from the laconic Jake.

Nancy

The Water Lily was at anchor when we reached the wharf, and a boat already rowing in to the landing. A minute later, just as I had expected, Joe was wringing me by the hand, as if he had a design on the continuity of my bones.

"Nancy's bad," he blurted out. "Won't you come and see her to oncet?"

I smiled in spite of my anxiety as I looked down at my trusty bag. "I'm all ready," I replied.

The deck of the schooner was crowded with people as we came alongside. The main hatch had been taken off, and the women and children had come up for an airing. They, like our friends, were taking their passages home from their fishing stations. They are known as "freighters."

"The skipper's been awful good, Doctor. When he heard Nancy were sick, he brought her out of t' hold, and give her his own bunk. But for that she'd have been dead long ago. She had t' fits that bad; and no one knowed what to do. She were ill when t' vessel comed

into t' harbour, and t' skipper waited nigh
three days till she seemed able to come along.
Then her got worse again. Not a thing have
passed her lips this two days now."

In the little, dark after-cabin I found the
sick girl, scarcely recognizable as the bonny
lass whose wedding we had celebrated the
previous winter with such rejoicings. There
were two young women in the cabin, told off to
"see to her," the kindly skipper and his officers having vacated their quarters and gone
forward for poor Nancy's benefit.

The case was a plain one. It was a matter of
life and death. Before morning a baby boy had
been brought into the world in that strange
environment only to live a few hours. The following day we ventured to move the mother,
still hanging between life and death, to the
hospital.

And now came the dilemma of our lives. It
was impossible to delay the schooner, as already the crowd on board had lost several
days; and it was not safe or right so late in the
year to be keeping these other families from

their homes. The Water Lily, so the kindly captain informed us, must absolutely sail south the following morning. My own vessel was in the same plight. We had more work outlined that we must do than the already forming ice promised to give us time to accomplish. To send poor Nancy untended to sea in a schooner was simply to sign her death-warrant. Indeed, I had small hope for her life anyhow.

Our hospital was on the coast of Labrador, and the remorseless Straits of Belle Isle yawned forty miles wide between it and the nearest point of the island home of most of our friends. One belated vessel, still waiting to finish loading, lay in the harbour. She expected to be a week yet, and possibly ten days if the weather held bad. An interview with the skipper resulted in a promise to carry the sick woman to her harbour if she were still alive on the day of sailing, or news of her death if she passed away.

Joe had no alternative. He certainly must go on, for he had nothing for the winter with him, no gear, and no way of procuring any. So it was agreed that Nancy should be left in our care, and, if alive, should follow by the schooner. Only poor Nancy was undisturbed next morning by the creaking of the mast hoops and the squealing of the blocks — the familiar warning to our ears that a vessel is leaving for sea. For she lay utterly unconscious of the happenings of the outside world, hovering between life and death in the ward upstairs.

To whatever cause we ought to ascribe it does not much matter. But for the time, anyhow, our arrangements "panned out right." The weather delayed the fish vessel till our patient was well enough to be moved. Ten days later, sewed up in a blanket sleeping-bag, Nancy was painfully carried aboard and deposited in a captain's berth — again most generously put at her disposal.

And so once more she put out to sea.

It was not until the next spring that I heard the final outcome of all the troubles. Nancy had arrived home in safety, with only one hitch — her kit-bag and clothing had been forgotten in sailing, and when at length she

Nancy

reached her harbour, she had had to be carried up to her home swathed only in a bag of blankets.

Such are but incidents like head winds in the lives of the Labrador fisher-folk; but those who, like our people, are taught to meet troubles halfway look at the silver lining instead of the dark cloud. As for Joe himself, he is still unable to get into his head why these events should be of even passing interest to any one else.

SALLY'S "TURNS"

"Spin me a yarn, Uncle Eph. I'm fairly played out. We've been on the go from daylight and I'm too tired to write up the day's work."

"A yarn, Doctor. I'm no hand at yarns," said the master of the spick-and-span little cottage at which I and my dogs had brought up for the night. But the generously served supper, with the tin of milk and the pot of berry jam, kept in case some one might come along, and the genial features of my hospitable host, slowly puffing at his pipe on the other side of the fireplace, made me boldly insistent.

"Oh, not anything special, Uncle Eph, just some yarn of an adventure with your dogs in the old days."

Uncle Eph ruminated for quite a while, but I saw by the solid puffs he was taking at his pipe that his mind was working. Then a big smile, broader than ever, lit up his face, and he said slowly:

"Well, if you're so minded, I'll tell you a

Sally's Turns

yarn about a fellow called 'Sally' who lived down our way in my early days."

At this I just settled down comfortably to listen.

Of course Sally was only a nickname, but on our coast nicknames last a man all his life. Thus my last patient, a woman of forty-odd years, trying to-day to identify herself, explained, "Why, you must know my father, Doctor. He be called 'Powder' — 'Mr. Powder,' because of his red hair and whiskers."

Sally's proper nickname was apparently "Chief," which the boys had given him because he had been a regular "Huck Finn" among the others. But in young manhood — some said it was because "Marjorie Sweetapple went and took Johnnie Barton instead o' he" — somehow or other "Chief" took a sudden "turn." This expression on our coast usually means a religious "turn," or a turn such as people take when "they sees something and be going to die"; it may be a ghost or sign. But this turn was neither. It was just a plain common "turn."

Labrador Days

It had manifested itself in "Chief" by his no longer going about with the other boys, by his habits becoming solitary, and by his neglecting his personal appearance, especially in letting his very abundant hair grow longer than fashion dictates for the young manhood of the coast. That was the reason some wag one day dubbed him "Absalom," which the rest caught up and soon shortened to "Sally." In the proper order of things it should have been "Abe." Was n't Absalom Sims always called "Abe"? There was obviously an intentional tinge of satire in this unusual abbreviation.

Whether it was due to the "turn" or not, the fact remained that at the advanced age of four and twenty Sally was still unmarried. He lived and fished and hunted mostly alone. No one, therefore, had much to say of him, good or bad. In its kindly way the coast just left him alone, seeing that was what he wished.

As the years went by it happened that hard times with a scarcity of food struck "Frying-Pan Tickle," the hospitable name of the cove where Sally was reared. Fish were scarce, cape-

Sally's Turns

lin never struck in, fur could not be got. This particular season every kind of fur had been scarce. A forest fire had driven the deer into the country out of reach. The young bachelor seals, called "bedlamers," that precede the breeding herd on their annual southern whelping excursion, and normally afford us a much-needed proteid supply, had evidently skipped their visit to the bay; while continuous onshore winds made it impossible in small boats to intercept the mighty rafts, or flocks, of ducks which pass south every fall. As a rule the ducks "take a spell" feeding off the shoals and islands as they go on their way, but the northeaster had robbed our larders of this other supply of meat, which we are in the habit of freezing up for spring use.

In spite of the ice jam, packed by the unfriendly winds, the men had ventured to set their big seal nets as usual, not expecting the long persistence of "weather" that now seriously endangered their recovery.

The time to move to the winter houses up the bay had already passed, and so the men at last thought best to go on and get them ready and then come out once more to haul and stow the nets and carry the women back with them. The long-delayed break came suddenly at last, with a blue sky and a bright, calm morning, but alas! no wind to move the packed-in slob ice. So there was no help for it but to get away early on shanks' pony, if they decided to go on; and that would mean they would not "reach down" before dark. There were only three of them, but they were all family men: Hezekiah Black, called "Ky"; Joseph Stedman, known as "Patsy," and old Uncle John Sanborne. They got under way bright and early, but the weather clouded up soon after they left, and a puff or two of wind should have warned them all under ordinary circumstances to abandon the attempt, or at least to branch off and take shelter in the "Featherbed Tilt" before trying to cross the White Hills.

As it was, Uncle John decided to adopt that plan, leaving the younger men, whom nothing would dissuade from pushing ahead. After

Sally's Turns

all, they knew every turn of the trail, every rock and landmark on the hillside; and one need not wonder if the modern spirit of "hustle" finds an echo even in these far-off wilds. Throwing precaution to the winds, the two young men pushed on regardless of signs and omens.

Sally just knew it. Nothing would ever convince him that they did not deserve to get into trouble for not respecting "signs." Even Uncle John had often talked about "t' foolishness o' signs," and many a time Ky, once a humble member of Chief's followers, had laughed at what he called "old women's stuff." But what Sally thought of signs would not have been of any interest in itself. The interesting thing was that though he was in the country hunting, having moved long ago to his winter trapping-grounds, he saw signs enough to make him anxious about the three fathers of families tramping over the bleak hills that day. When snow began to fall with a westerly wind, that was sign number one. Something uncanny was about to happen. Then there was sign number two of bad weather coming, namely, the tingling in his fingers and sometimes "a scattered pain in t' joints." So Sally left his fur-path for the day, hurried back to his tiny home among the trees, and, calling his dogs together, harnessed them quickly and started at once for the winter houses at the bottom of Grey Wolf Bay.

A tenderfoot could have told now that they were "in for weather." The snow by midday was not falling, it was being shovelled down in loads. The temperature had dropped so rapidly that the flakes, as large as goose feathers, were dry and light, a fact that with the increasing wind made the going like travelling through a seething cauldron. Unfortunately the men were already over the crest of the White Hills when they realized that the storm which had swept down on them had come to stay. There was no stemming the gale on the wind-swept ice of those hillsides, even could they have faced the fiercely driving snow. All they could do was to hurry along before it, knowing there would be no shelter for them

Sally's Turns

till they reached Frying-Pan Tickle. For the forest had retired there beyond the hills before the onslaught of man and the carelessness that had caused forest fires.

No one who has not been through it has any conception of the innumerable little accidents which in circumstances like these eat up the stock of chances for coming through. It did seem foolish that Patsy got his mittens wet in salt water coming through the broken ballicater ice as they tried to make the short cut across the Maiden's Arm; and that they froze while he was trying to warm his hands, so that he could not get them on again. It sounds like madness on Ky's part to have let his nor'-wester cap get blown away, but it really only fell from his numbed hands while he was knocking the snow off, and was instantly swept away in a flurry of snow in the darkness. When the beam broke in his snow racquet, one of a pair he had absolutely counted on as beyond accident, he could scarcely get ahead at all.

To stop and try to "boil the kettle" would not only have occupied too much time, but under the circumstances making a fire was practically impossible. Neither of the men carried a watch, and the unusual darkness caused by the thick snow made it impossible for them to tell what progress they were making. They supposed that surely between the worst snow "dweys" they would catch sight of some familiar leading mark, but that proved only another of their small but fatal miscalculations. The storm never did let up. More than once they discovered they were out of the track, and, knowing well their danger, had grudgingly to sacrifice time and strength in groping their way back to a spot where they could recognize the trail again.

December days are short, anyhow, "down north" and every moment warned them that the chances of getting out before dark were rapidly diminishing. All the strength and endurance of which they were capable were unstintingly utilized to get ahead; but when night finally overtook them, they knew well that there were several miles to go, while to move ahead meant almost certainly losing the

Sally's Turns

trail, which inevitably spelt death. It was only
the winter before that Jake Newman, of Rog-
ers Cove, left his own home after dinner, "just
to fetch in a load of wood," and he was n't
found till three days later, buried in snow not
two hundred yards from his front door, frozen
to death. But if to advance meant death, to
stop moving was equally dangerous. So there
was nothing to do but keep moving round and
round a big rock in hopes of living out the long,
terrible night.

Meanwhile Sally was under way. Though he
knew that the men were crazy to get back, it
was only his surmise that they had started, so he
had to call round at the winter cottages in the
bay to make sure. He realized full well it was
a man's job he was about to undertake, and
had no wish to attempt it unnecessarily. As
he expected, however, he found that the
houses were all shut up, and such tracks as
there were on the snow about the trail end
showed quite clearly three men's footmarks.
"Uncle John's gone with t' others," he muttered to himself. "I 'low 't is t' last journey

some of 'em'll make, unless they minded the signs before too late. 'T is lucky that I had n't left old Surefoot at t' tilt; more'n likely I shall be needing he before t' night's out." And he called his one earthly chum and constant companion to him, rubbed his head, and made him nose the men's tracks which he was about to follow.

In spite of his nickname, Sally was no greenhorn on occasions like this. Every harness was carefully gone over, every trace tested; the runners and cross-bars of his komatik all came in for a critical overhauling. The contents of the nonnybag were amply replenished; the matches in the water-tight bottle were tested for dampness; his small compass was securely lashed to the chain of his belt. His one bottle of spirits, "kept against sickness," was carefully stowed with the tea and hardtack. A bundle of warm wraps, with his axe, and even a few dry splits, completed his equipment. Then once more Surefoot was shown the tracks on the threshold, the trailing loops of the traces were hitched on their respective toggles, the stern line was slipped, and away went his sturdy team into the darkness.

That animals have a sense of direction that man has lost is clearly proven by the seals, birds, polar bears, and our northern migratory animals generally, who every year follow in their season the right trails to their destinations, even though thousands of miles distant and over pathless seas or trackless snows and barrens. That instinct is nowhere more keenly developed than in our draught dogs; and amongst these there are always now and again, as in human relationships, those that are peerless among their fellows. Surefoot's name, like Sally's own, was not strictly his baptismal cognomen, the original name of "Whitefoot" having been relegated to oblivion early in life owing to some clever trail-following the pup had achieved.

Many men would face an aeroplane flight with a sinking sensation. Many would have to acknowledge some qualms on a start with "mere dogs" in a blizzard like this one. But Sally, unemotional as a statue and serene as a judge, knew his pilot too well to worry, and, stretched out full length on the sledge, occupied himself with combating the snow in between "spells" of hauling the komatik out of hopeless snowbanks. "It won't do to pass the Featherbed without making sure them's not there," thought Sally. "If Ky had any wits about him, he'd never try the Hanging Marshes a night like this." So when at last the team actually divided round the leading markpole, Surefoot having rubbed his side on it, so straight had he travelled even in that inferno, Sally leaped off immediately, and, following the line of poles, was cheered to see sparks issuing from the snug tilt among the trees. But alas, there was only one man, old Uncle John, resting there safely when Sally came tumbling in. The cheerful wood fire, the contrast of the warmth and quiet with the howling and darkness of the storm outside, called loudly to every physical faculty to stay for the night.

"Where be them gone?" queried Sally as soon as the old man had roused himself enough to understand the sudden interrup-

Sally's Turns

tion. "Where's Ky and Patsy? I thought you was all together by t' tracks."

"So we was, so we was, boy. But them's gone on, while I thought I'd bide till daylight."

The loud wail of the dogs in chorus, as they chafed at being left out of sight or knowledge of their master's whereabouts, was plainly audible to both men, and suggested the cruel bleakness of the night outside.

"Youse isn't going on to look for 'em, is you? There be no chance of doing nothing a night like this," added the old man.

But Sally was in another world. He could see the two men adrift and trying to keep life in themselves on the White Hills just as plainly as the cry made him see his beloved dogs calling to him from the exposed trail outside.

"There'll be nothing left anyhow to do by morning, Uncle John," he answered. "Look after yourself well and keep t' fire in; maybe I'll be back sooner than us expects. Good-night to you." And Sally disappeared once more into the night.

They were still alive when Surefoot found

them, though far more played out than one would suppose strong men could be in so short a time. The extra wraps were at once requisitioned, a ration from the spirit flask was rapidly given to each, and then, forcing them to sit down on the sledge, Sally again encouraged Surefoot to take the trail. Downhill, they managed to move along, but the heavy thatch of snow made progress difficult on the level and almost impossible uphill, just when exhaustion made marching impracticable even with a line from the sledge lashed to their arms. Sally found his last device unavailable. The men must get off for the uphill work, and that is what it became increasingly impossible for them to do.

Apparently Ky was the worse off. He did n't seem to know what was going on. Sally noticed that his hat had gone and thought his head was freezing, so without hesitation he covered it with his own warm nor'wester. Ky lay mostly on the komatik now, and it took all Sally's strength and such little aid as Patsy could give to enable the dogs to haul up the

Sally's Turns

Frenchman's Leap, usually nearly perpendicular, but now fortunately sloped off by the heavy drift. Each man had to take a trace ahead and haul exactly like two big dogs, thus strengthening the team. At last the komatik topped the brow and was once more coming along after them. But Patsy was so played out that Sally drove him back to the sledge, hoping that the dogs could now haul the two men again. To his horror on reaching the komatik he found the real cause of its running so much more easily. Ky was gone. Probably he had only just slipped off. He would go back and look for him. But then he would lose the dogs. Patsy was too lost to the world to understand anything or to help. If he went back alone the dogs might follow and he would lose Patsy as well. Still he must try it. Halting the dogs he turned the komatik over, driving the upturned nose of the runners deep into the snow; then he laid Patsy on the top, and, lashing him on, finally began groping back down the steep rise for the missing man.

Not a sign was to be found; any traces he

had left were not only invisible, but impossible to feel, though he took off his mittens to try. The pitiless, driving snow instantly levelled off every mark. How long dare he delay? He remembered at last that even if he found him he could do no good. He could never carry him up the hill. But he had tried — had done his best and his conscience felt easier. And then there was Patsy. He might save Patsy yet. It was right he should go on. Fortunately the dogs were giving tongue when he crawled and stumbled once more up the Leap. They knew their master had left them and had come back to the komatik to wait. Some of them were huddled up against the motionless body of the man. Surefoot, bolt upright on the topmost bend, was leading the chorus. The komatik had to be extricated and righted. Patsy was still breathing. His body must be re-lashed on the right side; and then once more the weary march began — the march that was a battle for every inch.

Of the remainder of the journey Sally never had much remembrance. It was like a moving

Sally's Turns

dream — he knew it was crowded with adventures, but the details had vanished completely from his ken. It was his old father who told the remainder of the story. He had turned into bed as usual, never dreaming any man was astir on such a night as that. He was sleeping the sleep of the righteous when he suddenly became conscious of dogs howling. Even dogs would not be out unless they were in harness on such a night. His own dogs he knew were safely barred into their kennels after being fed at sundown. For a few minutes he lay awake and listened. The sounds came no nearer, but they were quite distinct. There was something astir in the darkness — something uncanny. Sally would have called it a "sign." Uneasily he arose and lit the lamp. He could not hear a soul stirring. Even the howling of the dogs had ceased. Nothing but the noise of the house creaking and groaning under the wind pressure was discernible. And then, just as the bitter cold, dark, and loneliness made him long to get into his warm bed again, the wail of a lone dog was distinctly audible. Uncle Eben, pulling the lamp safely out of the draught, opened a crack of the porch door only to be saluted by a rush of cold wind and snow which nearly swept him off his feet. But again clearer than before came the wail of the dog.

"He must be hitched up by mistake or in harness," he thought. "I 'low I'll fire a powder gun."

Going back into the bedroom, the old man warned his wife that he was going to shoot and not to be frightened. Then taking his old muzzle-loader, which was always kept ready, from among the lesser weapons which stood in the gun-rack, he poked the muzzle through the crack and fired it into the air. True he had thought there might be some one adrift. But even a prophet could not have imagined that what did happen could have done so. For the sound of the explosion had not done echoing through the empty rooms before the door was burst suddenly in by some heavy body falling against it. The thud of some weighty mass falling on the floor was all that Uncle Eben could make out, for the gust through the wide-

open door at once extinguished the light. It
seemed as if some huge bird must have been
hovering overhead and have fallen to the
charge of the big gun. The door must be shut
at all costs, and shut at once; so Uncle Eben,
stooping to feel his way over the fallen object,
put his hands out to find where it lay in the
darkness. Instantly he recognized the body of
a man — a man alive too, but apparently unable to speak or move. Like lightning he had
the door closed. The vigour of youth seemed
to leap into his old veins. The light was soon
burning again, to reveal to him the prostrate
body of his own son, ice-covered from head
to foot, his hatless head like a great snow
cannon-ball, his face so iced up that it
was scarcely recognizable. No — he was un-
wounded and there was life in him. "I had
just to thaw his head out first," Uncle Eben
said, "and then us rubbed him and got something down his throat. He roused himself, got
up, and told us his dogs must be snarled up in
t' woodpile on the hillside, only a few minutes
away, and he kept signing that there were

a man, possibly still alive, lashed on t' komatik." It was no night for the old man to go out. "He'd be dead, bless you," before he got anywhere; and it seemed impossible to let Sally go out again. The stranger must surely be dead long ago. But, weak as he was, Sally would go. He could stand now and was once more blundering toward the door. To live and think he had let a man perish alongside was as impossible to one man as to the other.

It was Uncle Eben who solved the problem. There were a dozen balls of stout seal twine lying in the locker. The old man, unable longer to haul wood or drive dogs himself, spent much of his time knitting up gear for the boys. He put on Sally his own cap, coat, and mits, tied the twine round his wrist, and then let him out to find the komatik again if he could; while if he fell exhausted Uncle Eben could at least follow the line and perhaps get him back again.

As events turned out they were justified in making the attempt. The cold wind served only as a lash to Sally's reserve strength and

his grit. That night he certainly found himself
again. He reached the sledge, cut the traces he
could not disentangle, and, keeping Surefoot
by him, he cleared the komatik of the woodpile. Once more he hitched in the dogs, which
he knew would make straight for the house,
while he piloted down that last hillside.

Patsy got well again, though his toes and
fingers alike were badly burned. Ky was not
found till a few days later. He had evidently
wandered to the edge of the cliffs, which near
the Jump fall perpendicularly a hundred feet
on to the rocky beach below, and had slipped
over in the darkness.

Uncle Eben's shot had passed almost immediately over Sally's head. He remembers
being unable to free the dogs, realizing he was
close home, and stumbling on for only a minute
or two before something exploded just above
him; then he recalls nothing till Uncle Eben
had thawed out the touselly head and rubbed
back the circulation into the frozen limbs.

The slur so obviously intentional in the old

nickname made it impossible for any one to use it longer. It was unanimously agreed that he had established most surely his right to his old name of "Chief," and by this for many years he was known. With the lapse of years and the advent of grey hairs, even that was gradually recognized as too familiar, and he received the cognomen of "Uncle," the title of endearment of the coast, attached to his own name of Ephraim. Moreover, this proved to be the last of Sally's "turns," for the long hair and the lonely habits disappeared. The barrier that had grown up between him and his fellows vanished, as they always do before the warmth of unselfish deeds — and the next time "Chief" asked a girl the fateful question, there proved to be no Johnnie Barton in his way.

"Is Sally living still?" I asked, my keenness of interpretation obscured by weariness or by interest in the details.

"Oh, yes, he's alive all right," replied my host — and my mind at once apologized, as I realized he had been telling me the story of his own early life.

THE DOCTOR'S BIG FEE

A CROWD of visitors had landed from the fort-
nightly mail boat, and had come up to see the
sights of our little harbour while our mails and
freight were being landed and the usual two
hours were allowed to collect and put aboard
any return packages or letters. The island on
which the station stands is a very small one,
attractions are naturally few, and custom has
reconciled us to the experience, strange enough
at first, of being included in the list of
"sights."

A nice, cheerful group had just "done the
hospital" and its appendages, and were resting on the rocky hilltop, after seeing the winter
dog-team and examining the hospital reser-
voir. The ever-recurrent questions had been
asked, and patiently answered — yes, the ice
was cold, but not always wet; the glare of the
snow was hard on the eyes; dogs do delight to
bite; and so on. Conversation flagged a little
till some one enquired the names of the head-

lands and bays stretching away in succession beneath our view.

"It all looks so grim and cold, and the people seem so scattered and so poor. Surely they can't pay a doctor's fees?" some one asked.

"That depends on what you mean by a fee. We don't expect to get blood out of a stone."

"Is all your work done for nothing, then?"

"No, not exactly for nothing. There is no produce of the coast which has not been used to express gratitude, and 'to help the hospital along.' Codfish is a common fee. Sealskins, venison, wild ducks, beadwork, embroidered skinwork, feathers, firewood — nothing is too bizarre to offer."

"Do they never pay money?"

"Yes, sometimes. Of late years, a little more each year. But when we began work, they practically never got any with which to pay. The fur-trading companies settled in kind, values were often measured, not by so many dollars, but by so many pelts. The traders gave out supplies on credit, took the fish or fur from their planters in return, and made up the bal-

The Doctor's Big Fee

ance, when there was any, in goods. Even barter was quite unusual, though some traders had a 'cash price' for produce paid down at once, besides the credit price."

"Do you think it a sound policy to be providing services, drugs, and nursing free?" chimed in a grey-bearded old fellow, evidently the philosopher of the party.

"Sometimes, sir, policies must be adopted which are rendered necessary for the time by conditions. Besides, as I have said, the people pay what they can, and, after all, it is they who catch the fish and fur, reaping harvests for the world's benefit — for not much return."

"Well, I'm glad that you don't do it for nothing, anyhow. That would be an imposition on the workers as well as on the subscribers."

The old gentleman seemed a bit disgruntled, so I ventured to put my viewpoint in a different way.

"Do you see that steep, rocky cape over there?" I asked. "It is the most northerly you can distinguish."

Labrador Days

"A great landmark, and worth the journey up here only to look at it," he answered with an enthusiasm which showed that he had a tender spot for Nature's beauties, and that even if the shell was hard, the kernel was soft.

"There is a little village just behind that head. It is hidden away in a rift in the mountain which forms a tiny cove for a safe anchorage. I had as big a fee there only two days ago as ever I received when I was practising in London."

The company looked up in astonishment, but like Brer Rabbit, I lay low to see if they cared for an explanation. I thought I saw a twinkle in my critic's eye as it caught mine.

"Go ahead," was all that he said, however.

Deep-Water "Crik," we call it. About half a dozen fishermen's families live there. Well, three days ago a boat came over at daylight to see if they could get a doctor, and I was debating as to the advisability of leaving the hospital, when an old skipper from a schooner in the harbour came ashore to tell me: "It's t' old

The Doctor's Big Fee

Englishman; Uncle Solomon they calls him. He's had a bad place this twelvemonth."

"How's the wind outside?"

"Soldier's wind. Abeam both ways."

"Think I could get back to-night?"

"Yes, by after dark."

"Let's get right away, then."

But other calls delayed us, and it was nearly midday before we started for the cape. Unfortunately, the wind veered as the sun sank, and "headed" us continually. The northern current was running strong, and it was just "duckish" when at last we entered the creek.

The former glories of Deep-Water Creek have passed away. Fortune has decreed that seals and mackerel and even salmon to a large extent should not "strike in" along that shore. Bad seasons and the wretched trading system have impoverished the fishermen, while the opening of the southern mines has taken away some of the most able-bodied. Here and there a braver cottage still boasts a coat of whitewash and a mixture of cod oil and red dust on the roof. But for the most part there is a sombre, dejected look about the human part of the harbour that suggests nothing but sordid poverty.

It had commenced to rain, and we were wet, cold, and feeling generally blue as we landed at a small fish stage, whose very cleanliness helped further to depress us, telling as it did the tale of a bad "voyage." For now it ought to have reeked of fish and oil; and piles of cod heads, instead of the cleanest of cold water, should have covered the rocks beneath. So many of our troubles are due to deficient dietary, winter was already on our heels, and there seemed to be the shadow of hunger in the very air.

As soon, however, as we landed, a black-bearded, bright-faced man of about fifty gave us a hearty greeting, and such evident happiness lit up his peculiarly piercing eyes that it made us feel a little more cheerful, even before he had taken us into his house. There we found a cup of steaming hot tea prepared. That tea did not seem a whit less sweet, because "there be ne'er a drop o' milk in t' harbour, Doctor, and molasses be scarce, too, till t' fish be dry."

Everything was so clean that you could have eaten off the floor. The pots and pans and tin cooking-utensils shone so brightly from the walls that the flame of the tiny kerosene lamp, reflected from so many sides at once, suggested ten hundredfold the candle-power it possessed. A museumful of treasures could not have added to the charm of the simplicity of the room, which, though small, was ever so cosy compared with the surroundings outside. Three children were playing on the hearth with a younger man, evidently their father.

"No, Doctor, they are n't ours exactly," replied our host, in answer to my question, "but us took Sam as our own when he was born, and his mother lay dead, and he've been with us ever since. Those be his little ones. You remember Kate, his wife, what died in the hospital?"

Yes, I remembered her very well, and the struggle we had had in trying to save her.

"Skipper John," I said as soon as tea was

over, "let's get out and see the old English-man. He'll be tired waiting."

"Youse need n't go out, Doctor. He be upstairs in bed."

So upstairs, or rather up the ladder, we went, to find the oddest arrangement, and yet far the most sensible under the peculiar circumstances. "Upstairs" was the triangular space between the roof and the ceiling of the ground floor. At each end was a tiny window, and the whole, windows included, had been divided longitudinally by a single thickness of hand-sawn lumber, up to the tiny cross-beams. There was no lofting, and both windows were open, so that a cool breeze was blowing right through. Cheerfulness was given by a bright white paper which had been pasted on over everything. Home-made rag mats covered the planed boards. At one end a screen of cheese-cloth veiled off the corner. Sitting bolt upright on a low bench, and leaning against the partition, was a very aged-looking woman, staring fixedly in front of her, and swaying forwards and backwards like some whirling Dervish. She ceaselessly monotoned what was intended for a hymn.

"The old gentleman sleeps over there," said the skipper with his head just above the floor level. He indicated the screened corner, and then bobbed down and disappeared, being far too courteous a man to intrude.

The old lady took no notice whatever as I approached. No head was visible among the rude collection of bedclothes which, with a mattress on the boards, served for the bed.

"Uncle Solomon, it's the Doctor," I called.

The mass of clothes moved, and a trembling old hand came out to meet mine.

"Not so well, Uncle Solomon? No pain, I hope?"

"No pain, Doctor, thank t' good Lord — and Skipper John," he added. "He took us in, Doctor, when t' old lady and I were starving."

The terrible cancer in spite of which his iron constitution still kept him alive had so extended its fearful ravages that the reason for the veiled corner was at once apparent, and also the effective measures for ventilation.

Labrador Days

The old lady had now caught the meaning of my presence. "He suffers a lot, Doctor, though he won't say it. If it was n't for me singing to him, I don't know how he would bear up." And, strangely enough, even I had noticed the apparent descent from an odd, dreamy state to crude realities, as the old lady abandoned her droning, and talked of symptoms.

"But, Aunt Anne," I said, "you can't keep it up all night as well as all day?"

"No, not exactly, Doctor, but I mostly sleeps very little." And to my no small astonishment she now shut up like an umbrella, and at once recommenced her mesmeric monotone.

When the interview was over, and all my notes made and lines of action decided, I still did not feel like moving. I was standing in a brown study when I heard the skipper's voice calling me.

"Be you through, Doctor? There be two or three as wants to see you," it said; but it meant, "Is there anything wrong?" The long silence might mean that the sight had been too much for me.

70

The Doctor's Big Fee

"There's no hurry, Doctor," it hastened to add, for his quick ear had caught the noise of my start as I came to earth again.

"What can be the meaning of it all?" I was pondering. Is there any more explanation to the riddle of life than to Alice in Wonderland? Are we not all a lot of "slithy toves, that gyre and gimble in the wabe" — or worse? Must we who love living only regard it as one long tragedy?

The clinic of Skipper John's lower room included one or two pathetic tales, and evidently my face showed discouragement, but I confess I was surprised when the last poor creature had left, to find my host's hand on my shoulder.

"You'll be wanting a good hot cup o' tea, I knows, Doctor. And t' wife's made you a bit o' toast, and a taste o' hot berry jam. We are so grateful you comed, Doctor. T' poor old creatures won't last long. But thanks are n't dollars."

At that minute his happy, optimistic eyes chanced to meet mine. They seemed like good, deep water, and just for a second the thought crossed my mind that perhaps he knew more of the real troubles of life than his intellectual opportunities might suggest.

"No, Skipper," was all I said. "We doctors, anyhow, find them quite as scarce."

"Well, Doctor," he added, "please God if I gets a skin t' winter I'll try and pay you for your visit, anyhow. But I has n't a cent in the world just now. The old couple has taken the little us had put by."

"Skipper John, what relation are those people to you?"

"Well, Doctor, no relation 'zactly."

"Do they pay nothing at all?"

"Them has nothing," he replied.

"Why did you take them in?"

"They was homeless, Doctor, and the old lady was already blind."

"How long have they been with you?"

"Just twelve months come Saturday."

"Thanks, Skipper," was all I could say, but I found myself standing with my hat off in the presence of this man. I thought then, and still think, I had received one of my largest fees.

TWO CAT'S-PAWS

JEAN MARQUETTE had nothing French about him but his name. Indeed "ne'er a word of French" could the old man remember, for he had lived for many years on the bleak, northeast side of Labrador; and few folk knew why, for all his forbears from sunny France had studiously avoided the Atlantic seaboard.

Over his evening pipe, when the sparkling forks of fire bursting from the crackling logs seemed to materialize before his eyes again the scenes of his venturous life in the wild, as if they had been imperishably imprinted in the old trunks which had witnessed them, the old *coureur de bois* spirit, and even accent, flashed out as he carried his listeners back into the gallant days of the men who founded the great *seigneuries* which still stretch along the thousand miles of coast from the barren Atlantic seaboard to the bold heights of Quebec.

In this country, only separated from the land of Evangeline by a few miles of salt water, one might reasonably suppose that the good folk would look to the soil and the peaceful pursuits of Arcady for at least some part of their daily bread. But, with the exception of a few watery potatoes, Uncle Johnnie had never "growed e'er a thing in his life." His rifle and axe, his traps and his lines, had exacted sufficient tribute from wild nature around him, not only to keep the wolf from the door, but to lay up in the stocking in his ancient French trunk dollars enough to give his only child, Marie-Joseph, quite a little dowry for that coast.

It had often been a puzzle to us why this lonely old man, with no one belonging to him but one unusually pretty daughter, should have migrated to the lonely North. He had been asked more than once what the reason was, but he had always put the curious off by saying, "Hunting must be a lonesome trade. You wants a lot of room to catch foxes."

But one night, when he was in a more communicative mood than usual, we got the whole story out of him.

Late one fall, when the southern fishing craft

Two Cat's-Paws

had gone south, and the ground was crisp with the first frost of winter, the lovely calm and sunny October morning had induced him to suggest to his wife that she should go over to the neighbouring island with their two elder children, a girl and a boy, and have a picnic, while they gathered some of the beautiful red cranberries to "stow away" for the winter. The baby girl, Marie, was left at home with the little servant maid. The children had jumped for joy at the idea, and early after breakfast he had rowed them across to the island, returning himself to finish loading his small schooner with the household goods and chattels which they must take up the bay to their winter home in the woods. So busy had he been with work that only as it came time to go off for the family did he notice how suddenly the weather had chopped around. A sinister northerly flaw was already rippling the surface of the hitherto placid sea; and Uncle Johnnie, accustomed to read the sky like a book, hurried as he seldom did to get the small boat under way. No one could have driven her faster than he drove her, and the pace satisfied even his uneasy mind. The "cat's-paw" had stiffened to a bitter blast behind him, and long before the boat reached the beach, it was difficult enough to look to windward. Hauling up the boat, he gave the familiar call which his wife knew so well; but no answer came to greet him. Following along the shore, and still finding no traces, he suddenly remembered that there was an old deserted house nearly a mile farther along, and incontinently he started to run as fast as he could in its direction. As he drew near, to his infinite joy he caught sight of smoke issuing from holes in the leaky roof. Calling as he went, he soon reached the cabin, to find the little party trying to dry themselves before a wood fire in the crazy stove, which had no funnelling, and was filling the hut with eye-torturing smoke.

"Come along, Mother," he cried. "There's no time to be lost. If we hurry, we may get over before dark."

A little delay was caused by the children, who were unwilling to leave even that pretence of a shelter; and more time was lost crossing the island, the children having to be carried most of the way. At last, having placed them all safely in the boat, Uncle Johnnie proceeded to launch her, and by wading into the water himself, succeeded in keeping them dry for the start. But the increasing sea soon made even that sacrifice of little avail, for broken water and driving spray, with the now heavily falling snow, soon soaked them through and through, at last half filling the boat itself with water.

Uncle Johnnie knew by instinct that it was now neck or nothing. He must get across that strip of water if human endurance could do it. So he kept on and on, long after he might have gone back, and put the boat before it once more to run for the island only after it was well dark, and he was being blown astern anyhow in spite of his best efforts. Nearing the shore, he had every reason to expect disaster, for the boat was now half filled, and he could see no place to make a landing. So as soon as his oars struck bottom he once more jumped into the water, and, holding the boat in his iron grip, he dragged it and its precious freight once more out of the furious violence of the sea.

The children by this time were quite unable to "travel"; so, sending his wife ahead, Uncle Johnnie struggled along with the little ones as best he could.

Alas, all of them were thoroughly beaten out. As he passed a big boulder halfway across the island which served as a landmark for the pathway, Uncle Johnnie found his poor wife lying in the snow, and already beyond any help he could give. Hurrying on to the cottage as best he could, he deposited the children, and once more fled out into the darkness for his wife, only to be, as he feared, too late, and to be obliged to leave her where she had fallen. Distracted as he was, he could only once more hurry to the hut, where again nothing but disaster awaited him. The place was flooded, the fire was out, no dry matches were left, and the little boy was already following his mother into the great beyond. Tearing off his coat and shirt, and pressing the little girl to his naked skin, he covered himself up again as best he could, and was actually able by moving about the whole night long, not only to keep himself alive, but to preserve the vital spark in his little daughter. Help came in the morning from the nearest neighbour some miles away, who had been given the alarm by the servant maid from his home. But there was still one more loss for him to meet, his little daughter failing to react to all their tenderest efforts to bring her back to life.

Before Marie was out of her teens, half the young bloods of the neighbourhood were courting around Uncle Johnnie's house. But none of them ever made any headway, for Uncle Johnnie clung to his one ewe lamb with almost childish dependence, and guarded her with all the wiles of his lifelong woodcraft.

" 'T is natural enough," thought young Ned Waring, "that t' old man don't want to part with she. For there be nothing else for he round here now. Every stone on t' beach reminds he of his terrible misfortune." He had said this often enough before, but one day it struck him —

Labrador Days

"When you wants to outwit a beaver, youse got to bank on dem t'ings that are real part of his make-up, and which he can no more help than a bear can help licking molasses. Fishing isn't as good as it used to be round here, and swiles [1] — well, there be'ant one year in a dozen when they comes in any quantity. I reckon I'll rig t' Saucy Lass for a longer trip t' year, and see what luck'll bring lower down t' Labrador."

So it came to pass that year that on a day in June, with his two brothers and a shipped "hand," Ned landed north of fifty-three in a lovely cove in some islands off the mouth of a long bay. Even as he passed in he had seen fish schooling so thick "you could catch 'em by the tails." His vessel safely anchored, he went ashore, much as did the old navigators in the brave days of the French explorers. No sign of human beings existed anywhere. Thick groves of evergreen trees covered all the slopes of the valleys which held the river in whose mouth they had anchored. But though signs of rab-

[1] Seals.

bits, foxes, and other game greeted their trained eyes, not a living animal was to be seen moving anywhere.

It so happened, however, that as they stretched themselves out on the brow of the hill before returning to their schooner, Ned chanced to disturb a large bee, which resented painfully the intrusion of these idlers on his labours. It was an insect rare enough on Labrador; so, taking the overture as a touch of personal interest rather than hostility, they christened their cove "Bumble-Bee Bight," and the home which they partly built before the winter drove them south again, "the Hive"; while for purposes of his own Ned left the island unnamed.

The trip proved a bumper one. They carried a full fare home; and big were the rumours which got around of the fisherman's paradise which Ned Waring had discovered. When the voyage was turned in, Ned was able to purchase every essential and many comforts for the new home in the North, and yet have a balance coming to him large enough to furnish him with the bravest winter outfit a young suitor could wish.

Uncle Johnnie was, however, all the time "one too many" for him as well as all the rest; and never was he able to catch Marie alone. Things went on uneventfully through Christmas and the New Year. The old man no longer drove dogs. He spent almost all his time pottering around his own house, now and again cleaving a few billets of wood; but to all intents and purposes he was hibernating like one of our Labrador bears.

When March month once more came around, the magic word "swiles" was whispered from mouth to mouth, and Uncle Johnnie woke up like a weasel when a rabbit is about. Every day he sallied up to his lookout on the hill, telescope in hand, at stated hours. But the hours were so timed that Marie could always go with him.

"Swiles" are second nature to most Labrador men. As for Uncle Johnnie, he would leave his Christmas dinner any time if any one came and called, "Swiles!" He would rather haul

Two Cat's Paws

a two-dollar pelt over "t' ballicaters" than make two hundred in any other way.

"So I reckoned," said Ned cannily, "one chance to make t' old man friendly was to put him in t' way o' doing again what he was really scarcely able to do any longer; and that was, to have as many notches on his gaff-stick for dead seals as any other man.

"It were, however, longer than I cares to remember now, before much of a chance come my way, but it come at last. T' spring had been that hard and that quiet that I 'lows us could have walked over to t' Gaspé shore if us had been so minded. T' standing ice never broke up from Christmas to April month; and there'd been ne'er a bit of whelping ice near enough to see with a spyglass, or a swatch big enough for an old harp to put his whiskers through. So when us woke one morning and found that t' sea had heaved in overnight unbeknownst to us, and that there was lakes of blue water everywhere, every man was out with his rope and gaff, as natural as a young duck takes to water.

Labrador Days

"That evening t' ice packed in again, and by nightfall it all seemed fast as ever. There was always a big tide made round Cape Blowmedown, and as t' land fell sharp away on each side of it, it were never too safe to go off very far on t' ice. But, that being a bad year, every man was on his mettle, and us all took more chances than was real right.

"From t' bluff of t' head Uncle Johnnie had spied old and young seals on t' ice before most of t' boys was out o' bed; and us had a dozen or so on t' rocks before t' others was out t' ice at all. As those near t' land got cleaned up, us went a bit farther out each time; and more'n one seal I did n't exactly see so's to give Uncle Johnnie a better chance, and to let me keep all t' time outside o' he.

"Just before it came dark and we was two or three miles out, t' wind shifted all of a sudden and came off t' land. Uncle Johnnie had a tow of three big pelts, and, believe me, heaven and earth would n't have made he leave them swiles behind. I'd left mine just as quick as I felt t' shift, and never let on I had any, so's I

Two Cat's-Paws

could rope up Uncle Johnnie's load and hustle him toward t' land. But t' ice was that hummicky it was an hour before us got near, and there we were, almost dark, t' ice broken off, driving along about twenty yards from t' standing ice almost as fast as a man could walk, and t' wind freshening every minute. There was about a mile to t' bill of t' Cape, and after that there'd be no hope whatever.

"Four years before Jim Willis and his brother Joe had been caught just t' same way. Joe had perished in his brother's arms next day after he'd carried him for some hours, and Jim had drifted ashore on t' second day with only a spark of life left in him.

"Every other man had been ashore and gone home for long ago, not knowing we was working outside, and only one chance were left for we. For t' gap of water was getting wider every minute, and there was n't a loose pan to ferry over on big enough to float a dog. So I shouted to Uncle Johnnie to run along t' ice edge back up the bay just as hard as he could go, and I'd jump into t' water and swim for t' standing ice edge. I never expected to get out again, but t' good Lord arranged it, I suppose, that I should strike a low shelf running off level with t' water, and by kicking like a swile, I was able to climb up and on to the ballicaters.

"There was always a boat hauled up on t' cape for men gunning to get birds or swiles, and t' only chance was to get there and launch her before t' ice passed out. T' rise and fall of t' tide had piled up t' ballicaters at t' foot of t' cliffs like young mountains, and it was already dark, too, while my wet clothes froze on me like a box. I reckon that saved my legs from being broken more 'n once, for I fell into holes and slid down precipices, and, anyhow, next day I was black and blue from head to toe — though for that matter I'd have been green and pink glad enough to have t' chance it gave me.

"Anyhow, I got t' boat in t' water at last, and pulled out toward t' floe, but ne'er a sign could I make out of Uncle Johnnie. There were n't a moment for waste, for spray was drifting over t' punt, and she was icing up that fast that if we lost much time I knew that it was good-bye to home for both of us. So I had to risk hauling her up on t' ice, while I ran along t' edge, shouting for all I knew. I had n't gone many yards before I stumbled right over t' old man. In t' dark he had slipped into a lake of water that had gathered on t' ice, and was about half-dead already. For I had been moving and had n't noticed t' time, and Uncle Johnnie had given out quickly, thinking I were lost, anyhow. Well, in t' dark it was not an easy job to half-carry t' old man back to where I'd left t' boat. But when you must 't is wonderful what you can do; and even dragging him were n't as hard as rowing ashore against t' wind.

"T' men thought us would never reach land, for t' ice made so fast on t' punt and oars, and us were carried well outside t' bill while I was getting Uncle Johnnie. When we did at last make t' standing ice edge, it would have been t' end again if Marie had n't been clever enough to go and rouse out t' boys, and come with them right to t' very edge of t' ice looking for us. And she had n't forgotten some hot stuff nor a blanket neither. She told us afterwards that she saw Uncle Johnnie perishing of cold away out off t' cape before she left t' cottage, just as clear as she did when t' boys hauled us out of t' punt.

"Uncle Johnnie pulled round in a day or so, but I pulled round early next morning, and those two days gave me t' first chance I'd had to get to windward of t' old man, and have Marie for an hour or two by herself.

"T' business soon blew over, as I knew it would, and what's more, Uncle Johnnie were no more for letting any one get Marie away from him than he'd been afore. Indeed, it seemed to me that it made him cling closer to she than ever; and I got real down-hearted when it come time to fit out t' Saucy Lass for North Labrador once more.

"Lucky for me, I'd made t' most of my time when Uncle Johnnie were ill, and talked many times to Marie about how her father might get young again if he could go where he could for-

Two Cat's-Paws

get the old scenes. So when we had had t'
schooner painted up and launched, and t' sails
bent and began getting firewood and things
aboard, I got her to talk to he about coming
along with we.

"I've often noticed how t' very things you
thought t' last on earth to happen come about
just as easy as falling off a log. When I went
over next morning to pretend to say good-bye,
Marie whispered in my ear, 'He really wants
to go. He only wants asking' — and before
night we had it all arranged. We was to fix up
t' hold for him and Marie, and they'd come
along and make a new home alongside us at
Bumble-Bee Bight.

"I won't trouble you with t' story of t' voyage down, only to say that we found that two
could play better than one at hide-and-seek.
When at last we anchored off t' river mouth,
Uncle Johnnie was fair delighted. Nothing
would satisfy him but he must choose a spot for
his new house right away. But meanwhile t'
cargo had to be stored in t' 'Hive' out o' t'
weather. Uncle Johnnie was always extra care-

ful about his things and would n't allow no one but he to handle 'em. So Marie went up to get a fire and tidy up, while t' old man handed t' things up to we. For my part I found that I had to stay up at t' 'Hive' and help arrange t' goods as they came along; and, 'lowing it might be t' last chance, for we'd be into t' fishery straight away, I up and asked Marie if it would n't be as well not to build another house after all. All I wanted was her to share t' house we'd built already; and Uncle Johnnie would be less lonesome than he'd ever been since his accident, because instead of losing one, he'd be getting two. I'm not telling you all what was said; as I'd told t' boys not to hurry with t' unloading, and Uncle Johnnie did n't get ashore till real late. By that time it was all fixed up, but nothing was to be said till the house was ready next night.

"When us come in together hand in hand that evening, Uncle Johnnie had started his pipe after tea. He guessed right away something was up, but maybe he had guessed something before. All he said was, 'Well, Ned, all my bridges is burnt behind me, as you know, anyhow, and if it had n't been for you, there'd be no need of asking any one for Marie, for I'd have been gone. So I can't well say no; and she might go farther and fare worse for sure. So I'll just leave it to Marie herself, and if she says so, so it shall be.'

"And that's all there is to tell about it. Sure people often wonders how others came to live 'way down on these lonesome shores. But Marquette Islands have given me fish and fur and good life, with ne'er a cent owing to any man, and there's four fine youngsters to help out when we can no longer fend for ourselves."

THE TRIPLE ALLIANCE

"THEY brought in a blind man last night," said the house surgeon. "It only seemed a case of starvation, so I did n't call you."

"Where is he from?"

"About thirty miles in the country down north somewhere. Apparently he has been living at the bottom of a bay 'way out of the line of the komatik trail. Formerly he could get firewood easily, and a few bay seals and game to live on. He seems too proud to let people know how badly off he was."

"What's the history?"

"He has a wife and two girls, who appear to be in almost as poor shape as he is himself. He has been gradually growing blind for some time, and was up here two years ago to see the eye specialist. His name is Emile Moreau."

"A Frenchman! Why, I remember the man perfectly. A slow-growing cerebral tumor."

He had been under observation for some weeks, and we had had to decide that he would not be benefited by an operation. So he went away, promising to return soon. But this is the way he had kept his promise.

A few minutes later I stood by the bedside of the blind Frenchman. The poor fellow was a skeleton, with the characteristic sunken face and fallen skin with which we are familiar in those living on what we know as "dry diet." He had nothing to say for himself except, "Times has been none too good, Doctor. It is a bad country when a fellow can't see where he is going. 'T is many an odd tumble I've had, too, knocking around." Emile had been away from France for many a long day, and the only English he had ever heard was the vernacular of our Northern Coast.

"How's your wife and the kiddies you told us about when you were here last time? It strikes me that they may have had a tumble too."

"Well, I 'lows, Doctor, them has been clemmed up on times. But, Jeanie, she never says nothing; she's that busy with t' things I can't do. She 'lowed she'd stay and mind t' children till I get better a bit. No, that's right. She has n't much grub. But us uses very little, and she never complains."

Two days later our good dogs brought in the rest of the family — the babes to the warm welcome and plenty at the Children's Home, while one of the pluckiest little women I have ever known, even in a country of brave and self-reliant women, was carried into the hospital partially paralyzed with beri-beri. She was so close to the gate from which there is no returning that it took our nurses six months to wean her back to another spell of usefulness.

It was no ordinary conundrum which vexed my mind when the house surgeon at last announced, "These Moreau patients are well enough to leave hospital," though I had realized that for good or evil the day was near.

Neither had said a word about the future. The worst feature of sending them out was the personal affection which their lessons in contentment had kindled in us. How could this helpless family ever hope to keep the wolf from the door. A council of war was called the same

The Triple Alliance

evening, and some neighbours who well knew the dilemma in which we found ourselves asked to be allowed to attend. There was an old shack in the compound in which some workmen had once been housed, and which had subsequently been used as a small storehouse. It was proposed, in the absence of funds, for all hands to assault this stronghold, and convert it as far as possible into a habitable home.

Thus came into existence what developed later into the general headquarters of the "triple entente."

To relieve the situation, one child was adopted by a childless, well-to-do neighbour, and the other was left for education and care with our little wards in the Home. Emile learned basket-work; Jeanie took in washing. The Moreau exchequer once more was in funds. But two difficulties soon presented themselves. There was a glut in our basket market, and Emile found life without being able to move out of the house almost more than a man born to the sea and the trail could

bear. Small dogs in civilization are wont to fill
this gap. But alas, "down North" small dogs
are taboo — their imperious Eskimo congeners
having decided against them.

There happened to be at this time also under
our care an Eskimo lad from the Far North,
whom we had picked up suffering with a form
of lung trouble which only the radical operation of collapsing one side of his chest wall
could relieve. The ribs had been removed. The
boy had recovered slowly; but, having only a
very limited breathing capacity, he had been
allowed to remain for the chores he could do.
Without kith, kin, or even fellow countrymen,
he was a veritable pelican in the wilderness
without any home attachments — and a very
serious problem to ourselves.

Emile could cut wood, being strong as a
horse and an excellent axeman; but he could
not find it alone. He could carry heavy packages, but he could not find his way. He could
haul water, but could not economically direct
his energies. Karlek's eyes were the best part
of him. So it came about that one morning on

The Triple Alliance

the way to the hospital I met Emile whistling like a newly arrived robin in spring, his hand on Karlek's shoulder, and on his back a heavy sack of potatoes which he was bringing up to the hospital kitchen from the frost-proof cellar in the cove.

It brought a smile to one's lips to see the nonchalance and almost braggadocio of his gait as he stepped out boldly, covering the ground at a speed which was itself a luxury to one so long cut off from that *joie de vivre* of a strong man. And more, it brought a smile to one's soul to see the joy of victory flashing in the features of the upturned face — the triumph of the man over the pitifulness of his sightless eyes. The international dual alliance was making its début on the field. The firm of Karlek and Moreau, Eskimo and Frenchman, had come to stay.

So time went on, cheerfully and even rapidly for all concerned — the Mission developing its labour-saving devices as the work increased, and the help of its friends made it possible. A water-supply system soon partially obviated the need for hauling barrels in the summer from our spring and puncheons on the dog sledges in the winter. A roadway and narrow-gauge railway track relieved us of the necessity of so much portage on men's backs; and a circular saw, run by a small gasoline engine, cut up our firewood with less waste and with more satisfactory results.

As with the basket market, so with the chore market, the ground was once more falling away from beneath our poor friends' feet. Only the indefatigable Jeanie held the household together, for in the heyday of the dual alliance's prosperity, the little daughter had been permitted to return to her parents from the Children's Home.

With the lapse of years, however, even if Emile could see no better with his eyes, his other faculties had developed so largely as to surrender to him again the joy of independence of outside help, and with characteristic self-reliance and optimism he once more tackled his own difficulties.

I was recently visiting a small cottage, built

The Triple Alliance

on a tiny ledge under the shadow of gloomy, high cliffs. It was far from any pathway and only approachable by stumbling over huge rocks — the débris of the crags behind. The hut had been built by a lonely old fellow who resorted to it in summer because it was right on the fishing-grounds, and he was getting unable any longer to face the long row to and from his house in the harbour. Nowhere in the world is the old adage concerning the birds of a feather truer than on this coast. The poorer and lonelier a man is, the greater is the certainty that some other poor and lonely person will seek the shelter of their poverty. Thus it had been with old man Martin.

One day there had appeared at the cottage door from twenty miles farther down the coast one-legged Ike, an irregular, angular youth, who, stumbling over the hillside, and magnified into portentous proportions by one of our Promethean fogs, had nearly scared the wits out of even my trusty dog team. Quite without invitation from old man Martin, one-legged Ike had come to stay. The proximity to the fishing-grounds suited this seafarer, who shared in every particular the limpet-like characteristics of Sinbad's Old Man of the Sea.

Anyhow, old Martin had never shaken him off, and had been heard to excuse himself by saying, "After all, he can sit in a boat as well as any of them with two legs." "Where there's room for one, there's room for two," is almost an axiom of life on these shores. In the lapse of time the old man had taken his last voyage, and Ike had come into full possession of the estate, living almost like Robinson Crusoe, cut off from his fellows by to him impassable barriers.

It was a reported lapse in some other portion of Ike's anatomy that had led me to scramble along the landwash to the cottage. The ice having broken up and gone out of the harbour, I should have considered longer the advisability of the trip, — for the morning frosts left the jagged rock masses at the foot of the cliff harbingers of ill omen to the traveller, — had it not been that his isolation might possibly make even trivial trouble serious. For he had come safely through so many scrapes, not a few being of his own making, that I had nicknamed him in my mind "indestructible Ike."

At last, congratulating myself that I had arrived without any untoward happenings, I rapped loudly on his door, expecting to hear his squeaky, perpetually broken voice bid me enter. Much to my surprise, therefore, the door opened itself, and smiling in the doorway stood our blind friend.

"Good Heavens! Emile, how on earth did you get here? And why did you ever want to come, anyhow?"

"Why, I thought it was a good plan for me to go fishing," he replied, addressing apparently a huge rock, so accurately poised over the hut that it suggested any moment an annihilating assault upon it. "Ike's going to be pilot and I'm to do t' rowing. We're to be partners for t' summer, and Karlek's going to look after t' family and help out when he can. It feels like being young again to be on t' water with a fishing-line. And, mind you, Ike knows a few tricks with a line that's worth more'n another leg to we, once we be on t' grounds. They all 'lows he be as good as t' next man for hauling in fish, so be as there's any around."

Ike's indisposition, as I had surmised, was not of a serious nature, and I learned subsequently that it was the proper ratification of the terms of the new triple alliance that had more to do with the sick call than any undue foreboding of impending dissolution on Ike's part. There had been some hitch in coming to terms, and Emile had put the only one point in them to his credit, when he saw through the trick, and "plumped for a magistrate," feeling also that he could trust me for more than mere legal technicalities.

It was obviously an offensive campaign on which I found them bent. Ike had himself carefully repaired the boat's structure, having always a keen eye to comfort and safety; while from Emile's hands I could see that the task of tarring their warship, owing to Ike's temporary indisposition and the need for immediate preparedness, had fallen to him. His only method for finding out where he had applied that hot and adhesive liquid had left very apparent evidences of both his energy and his zeal. To Emile also had fallen the rearrangement of the big rocks, so as to form as level a surface as possible on which to dry the fish. It was a Sisyphean task, and poor Emile had spent much sweat and not a little blood in his efforts. But, as Ike told him, "lifting rocks were n't no work for a man with one leg." So he had offset against it getting the meals ready, and what he called "tidying things up." But as Karlek was, unrewarded, to bring the bread, Ike's household labours did not promise to be onerous.

In one sense the entente campaign proved victorious, for they had a goodly catch; but in the division of the spoils it apparently turned out that it had been so arranged that Emile's share was to catch the fish, Karlek's to dry it, and Ike's to exchange it piecemeal for tobacco or "things for t' house," as he called them.

Labrador Days

Ever since Stevenson wrote of the one-legged rascal Silver, one associates with that handicap a tendency to try to outwit others; while the dependence of blind men presupposes simplicity and trustfulness.

Emile worked like a tiger, with the single-mindedness of the Verdun spirit of France, blissfully supposing that Ike did the same in his end of the boat. Fishing in sixty fathoms of icy water, Emile would haul his lines up and down, re-bait and tend them, till his hands were blue with cold, and the skin "fair wore off t' bones." One day, however, a harbour trap boat happened to pass close by their rodney while they were anchored on the fishing-grounds, and the owner called out, "Wake up, Ike! Price of dream fish is down." Ike had somewhat loudly and not too politely responded to the salutation, but all the same it awoke a first suspicion in Emile's mind. While not slacking himself, he "kept an eye" on his partner as best he could.

He knew that a one-legged man must sit down for work, while for his part he stood, but he had not realized that Ike considered any more restful posture essential. "A blind man sees more'n most folk" is a common claim of Emile's. It is tedious pegging away when fish are scarce, yet fishing is a trade where "'t is dogged as does it." He suspected that Ike took it easy in the stern while he worked in the bow; and his doubts were confirmed when one day, from a passing boat, some one called out: "'T ain't safe for you to be out alone, Emile. You'll be running some one down one of these days." It was obvious that Ike was not visible over the gunwale.

From that day on, Emile began to count his catch and to put a cross-thwait in the middle of the boat to keep them separate — "Something to push my feet against when I rows, I called 'un," he told me. Still Ike was almost too much for him, for Karlek remembered seeing him sorting out the fish as he landed them, and the big ones, somehow or other, all found their way into Ike's yaffles. Ike also discovered that it was good economy constantly to change the location of such things as the tobacco box, butter tub, and molasses jar, for it often meant that the good-natured Emile went without.

The cold weather set in early, and though the contract was not up, Ike's hereditary instinct that hardship was bad for his constitution made him decide to stop if he could. But Emile went steadily on, having learned from Karlek that there were occasional leakages from the fish pile. He ventured to remonstrate with his partner, but as fish were plentiful, he refused to cancel the contract before the proper date.

It was Ike who finally forced the issue. Emile being bowman, it was their custom always to come in to the ladder leading to the stage platform head on, when Emile, grabbing the cross-bars with one hand and holding the painter in the other, climbed up and "made her fast." Projecting from the stage head is a long pole used for preventing boats that are made fast from bumping against the stage. Coming in a day or so later, Ike drove the punt in parallel with the stage head, and the pole coming into Emile's hands deceived him into thinking that the stage was above him as usual.

The Triple Alliance

He promptly stepped off the boat, and naturally fell into the water. Naturally also, it shook Emile up a good deal, for he was in the water quite a while. After the incident Ike's tender heart had made him absolutely refuse the responsibility of a blind man in a small boat in fall weather. As we walked up the wharf together Emile told me many more such details of the transactions of our only "triple alliance." All he wanted me to do was to add up his own tally of the fish he had caught, multiplying it by a reasonable average fish, and for the sake of the family help him to get from his ally a return for his labour which would enable him to buy food for the winter for Jeanie and the little girl.

Fortunately it proved to be not too late. You cannot "get the breeks off a Highlander," and after a week or two not a cod tail or a cent would have been available from Ike. As it was, my coming to the assistance of my poor friend happened to save the "entente" from being a tragedy, and enabled us to relegate the whole incident to our comedy group.

Labrador Days

A peremptory order to Ike to wait for me at midday at the room we call the court-house would, I knew, impress him with the necessity of obedience, far more than a second visit to his cabin. The effort which the journey would cost him and the time allowed for reflection would, moreover, punctuate the importance of the occasion.

Emile's calculation of the amount of fish caught, corrected by Karlek by the simple process of multiplying the sum by two, and with a bit more added by myself to be sure not to underestimate it, formed all the legal data I needed. The lean, scrawny figure of Ike, twisting and squirming with evident uneasiness, awaited my arrival at the appointed time. Ike's fear of "t' Law" was the superstition of a child. It was to him a great big man waiting to pounce upon you and "lug youse away." Indeed, I learned afterwards that he had stayed in bed for fear of being carried off surreptitiously. "'T is a lonesome spot I lives in," he had explained.

"To steal from a blind man, Ike," I began,

The Triple Alliance

"is bad. Moreover, it does n't bring any one any luck ever. Where have you put those sixty quintals of fish which belong to Emile?"

"It took more 'n half t' voyage, believe me, Doctor, to meet t' summer's expenses. There was n't more 'n thirty quintals all told, and half of that was mine. Samuels only allowed we four dollars a quintal, and his flour was eight, and molasses seventy cents. He said he 'd land Emile's share when he comes in on his home trip."

"The Law will have to send down and search your house and all around it, and carry off things while you wait here, and you won't get any credit for it either. I told you there was no luck for those who rob a blind man, unless they confess in time. I 'll come back in half an hour for your decision." And, having an unfair advantage of a one-legged man, I locked the door and was well down the road before Ike had made a move.

Our little rickety court-house, in order to be in the centre of the village, stands on a rocky hill-crest away by itself. When the wind blows high, awesome noises with much creaking and groaning help to suggest to the guilty conscience that supernatural agencies are at work. The half-hour was purposely a long one, and had the desired effect. Ike made a full confession of his delinquencies and promised reparation. An immediate search while he was in this frame of mind revealed that Emile's winter food could only be obtained by leaving Ike to a diet of hope and charity. The lesson being necessary, however, the whole of his supplies were loaded into the boat, and Ike condemned to row it to Emile's house and land it at once. It was late and dark, but the fear of what might happen to him alone on his point, now that it was known that he had robbed a blind man, held more terrors even than hunger for Ike. So the judgment of the court was carried out that very night.

Partly moved by curiosity, Christmas found me once again visiting the mansion under the cliff. A shortage in the commissariat was, I knew, no new experience to the poor fellow, and even the wiles of a " one-legger" cannot

The Triple Alliance

convert stones into bread. Ike, radiant with smiles and fat as a spring seal, was out to meet me on my arrival — which circumstance was a little difficult at first to understand. Then he explained:

"You'm right, Doctor. It drives away t' bad luck when you pays up a blind man. I has n't wanted ne'er a t'ing since."

It had been a good voyage that year, and, as a matter of fact, every one had a warm spot somewhere in his heart for "that rascal Ike." For though he was admittedly a rogue, he was always such an amusing, hail-fellow-well-met rogue, and not the really mean type which every one dislikes. All the shore had heard of his dilemma, and, isolation not allowing one man to know what another is doing, indiscriminate charity had poured in upon poor Ike, without possibly doing him much harm, for he attributed it absolutely to that oftentimes useful mentor of the feeble-minded, the great god of good luck.

To my surprise it was Emile who really suffered most, though he would not admit it, but

Labrador Days

by actual computation of the supplies in his
very give-away storeroom, I learned that he
had secretly carried back to Ike's beach in the
dark just one half of those goods which "t'
Law" had recovered for him; and which Ike
to this day believes were deposited for his
benefit by the good-luck fairy.

PORTLAND BILL

"It must be nigh sixty years ago, but I remembers it as if it was yesterday, when a new settler come to live in our harbour," said Skipper Life Flynn, at whose house I was spending the night with my driver and dogs.

"Life" was short for Eliphoreth — the "given" names being mostly out of the Bible down North. "It were a wonderful thing them days, for Father were the only Liveyer then — that is, as stayed all the year round. He did n't mind being alone, and t' moving in t' schooner every spring and fall were bad for Mother. Fish were plenty every season one side or t' other of Deadman's Cape, and there was lots of fur and swiles t' winter. So he built a house in Sleepy Cove, and there us grew up!

"No, Doctor, I'm not able now to read and write. None of us is, for us had no teachers. But we was all big, strong men, and handy at that, and there was n't a thing to be done wi' axe or saw about boats and timber us could n't do. We made a good deal at furring, too, and many's and many's t' night in winter I've laid down under t' trees and slept — with ne'er a greatcoat neither. An' if us was n't brought up scholars, Father taught us to be honest, and to fear God and nothing and nobody else.

"It were our way them days to greet every stranger as a friend, and so when Bill started his cabin, — for that was all it ever were, — us lads all went in and helped him chop and saw t' logs for studding.

"In winter Father minded t' big French Room; but he were away hunting most of t' time, there being no need to watch much, being as there was no one besides ourselves anywhere near. But early spring and late fall when t' fleets were passing, it were day and night watch, and not without a gun neither.

"But it would have paid us better to have watched that winter; for when t' Frenchmen come in t' spring there was a number of little things missing that Father had to stand to — and, somehow, us never suspected t' newcomer.

Portland Bill

"It was only long afterwards us learned how t' new settler come by his name— which was 'Skipper Bill Portland.' Seems that's where the big English convict prison is. So after Bill escaped, he not being good at letters, and not wanting exactly to use his own name, he just twisted her round, and to this day no one's ever found out really who he was before.

"Hundreds of schooners anchored in the Bight in our harbour that spring, t' whitecoats having come right in on t' floe, just t' other side of t' Deadman's Cape. One day a schooner captain read we a piece in t' papers about a man what had been a pirate, what had escaped to Newfoundland; and a hundred dollars was being offered for his head. Reading about that man made us all think of Skipper Portland. It were his build and his kind, too. But us folk never mixed with that kind of work; and all us did was to keep a good lookout for t' future. But a poor neighbour he proved to be, for he were as cute as a fox, and he had no fear o' nothing.

"He were n't no idle man, though, Skipper

Bill were n't. That second winter he set to and built a ten-tonner all by hisself — that is, t' hull. He had galvanized fastenings for her, such as he never bought fair in Newfoundland. But o' course he had no gear to fit her out, and he could n't get any more than he 'd got already off our room. We lads saw to that, and he knew it, too — and that it were n't safe playing no games, neither.

"He were away t' following winter, 'furring,' so he told we, but no fox could ever get fooled by a trap Skipper Bill set. It were n't in his line, getting round animals. Beyond which he had ne'er a trap. He 'lowed he just set deadfalls — a good name for his work, I'm thinking now. Anyhow, he came back with enough gear, stolen off French Rooms to t' south, I reckon, to get his boat afloat by t' time t' owners got back.

"She were an odd craft, built for a crew of one man only. For Skipper Bill had n't much trust in any man 'cept hisself. Once when he were full o' French brandy he told me that when he were working on t' cliffs in England, he found out that his mate were going to 'squeal,' as he called it, about his leaving, so he'd given him such a kick behind when he were n't expecting it that no one had ever heard from him since. He meant, we reckoned, that t' poor fellow had fell off t' bill into t' sea.

"When he built that boat he were thinking already that he might have to leave sudden, and perhaps a crew would n't be willing to, even if he got one. So he trimmed his teller lan-yards to run forrard, so as he could steer before t' foremast, and handle t' headsheets hisself going to windward, and at t' same time keep a lookout for ice and slob.

"Many's t' time I've seen him sailing along with ne'er a watch on deck at all, he being be-low aft steering by compass from t' locker, with t' tiller lines leading down the companion hatch.

"I minds one fall that he brought in a big cask o' rum and a lot o' brandy, which he were going to sell to us folk. But Father would n't stand for that. He said that he'd seen too much of it when he were young to want any more lying round. We lads found it only fun to go over and knock t' heads in, and hear what old Portland had to say about we.

"One day, however, a fellow all dressed in blue came down from St. John's to take he along, and before Bill knew it t' boat were alongside his craft and t' man calling he to come ashore. Bill knowed what he were at once. He'd had experience. 'All right, Officer,' he said, 'I'll just get my coat and come along.' But when he come up on deck he had a barrel of gunpowder all open and a box of matches in his hand. 'Come on, now,' he shouted with an oath, 'let's all go to hell together.' But just as soon as ever t' small boat backed off, he runs forrard and slips his cable, and was off before t' wind before youse could say 'Jack Robinson.'

"He always left his mainsail up, Skipper Bill did. 'Better be sure than sorry' was a rule he always told us were his religion.

"T' policeman seemed in two minds about following t' boat, but when she rounded Dead-man's Cape, he rows back ashore. I minds running up t' hill to watch where Skipper Bill would go, but he stood right on across for t' Larbadore. T' policeman said that that were n't his beat; and he looked glad enough that it were n't neither. Old Portland never came back to Sleepy Cove to live. He just left everything standing — which were mostly only what he could n't take away with him anyhow.

"That fall one of t' Frenchmen stowed away in t' woods when their ship was getting ready for home. His name was Louis Marteau; and his vessel had no sooner gone than in he goes and lives in Bill's house across t' cove. Things got missing again that winter, and though Father had to feed him, seeing that he had n't been able to steal a diet, we lads give him notice to quit in t' spring. As he did n't show no signs of moving, us just put a couple of big trees for shoes under t' house, and ran it and Louis, too, out onto t' ice as far as t' cape — a matter of two miles or more.

"So us thought us had done with both of them, and a good riddance too; but when t' spring opened t' Frenchman wrote up to t' English man-o'-war captain to come in and find out about t' things what they'd lost. So one day in comes t' big ship and anchors right alongside in our bay. T' very first man to come rowing across and go aboard to see what he could get, I reckon, was Louis Marteau. When t' captain asked him what he wanted, he said that he had come over to ask him to send a boat to t' cape to search his rooms, as t' neighbours blamed he for having taken their things.

"Well, it were a long way to go and there were no motor boats them days; and t' captain must have thought if Louis had taken anything he had it hid away where no one would find it. So they just did n't take t' trouble to send out a crew and look. At the same time Louis had stolen fish drying on his flakes, and stolen twine right in his open fish stage to go and catch more with.

"Another steamer came in t' fall, and Louis, thinking that t' trouble had blown over, went aboard as usual. One of t' officers, thinking that the man was just a fisherman, and as simple as most o' we, asked him if he did n't know where a man called Louis Marteau was. 'Yes,' said Louis, 'I knows he well. He be here to-day, and gone to-morrow' — and with that he slips away, and was far enough in the woods for safety long before the searching party landed.

"Louis, like old Bill, was as fond o' liquor as a cat is o' milk; and when he got French brandy in him, he did n't care what he did. There be only one law here which every one keeps, as you knows, Doctor, on this coast. Whatever else you does, you must never touch t' property of another settler, whether he be good or bad, or whether he be away fishing, or whether he be in America. Because any time he may need to come back, and that many are away summers fishing, if they can't leave their homes locked and feel 'em safe, they can't live at all. So everybody minds that law, whether it be written in St. John's or not. There are new stages, yes, and houses, too, and plenty of 'em, and boats hauled up, that men has left and gone to Canada years ago. They're tumbling down right alongside folk as needs 'em as bad as gold just for firewood, but ne'er a stick is touched come year, go year — not till they rots or t' sea comes and carries 'em away.

"Well, Louis and a man called Tom Marling got some liquor aboard that day, and started scrapping, Marling saying that Louis must be a crook or he would n't steal another man's house. T' end of that was that Louis shot Marling through the shoulder and nearly blew his arm off.

"Next spring a large bully sailed across t' Straits and four men landed in my cove. It chanced that old Skipper Sam Brewer caught sight of 'em, and he recognized Bill Portland from t' old days. T' other three was Tom Marling's brothers. All t' men had guns, and old Skipper Sam guessed they was after Louis. So he sent off his lad Mose to run out to t' cape and give he warning. Though why he should I can't say. Louis just said, 'All right, I'll be ready for 'em, boy,' and started right in loading his two big guns and his rifle. Then he fixed up t' windows and barred t' door, and when Mose come away he could see Louis moving round inside and swearing enough to frighten t' fish off t' coast for t' whole summer. Mose waited round out of sight all day to see what would happen. But nothing did, only before dark he saw the four men making their camp-fire on the edge of the woods near Louis's house. I reckon they knew he'd be ready and wanted to keep him waiting. Anyway, they was there all next day.

"T' third morning I caught sight of some men loading a boat at Louis's stage, so, being only a hobbledehoy then, I guessed they'd not take much notice of me, and no more they did. They told me Louis had tried to break away t' second night in t' dark, but they caught him and carried his pack back for him, and what else they did to he I don't rightly know. Any-how, they loaded up their own boat and then Louis's two boats with fish and twine, and everything else that were worth taking and they could stow, not forgetting t' barrel of flour and t' keg of molasses.

"Skipper Bill told me that t' Governor of-fered to make him t' captain of a man-o'-war, just to stop t' law-breaking on the coast. But

he were a policeman instead because he felt
ashamed to see t' laws broken and villains like
Louis go free. 'It's to teach you people on t'
coast to be good boys what brings us away
from our homes so far in t' fishing season.'

"They never stopped loading a minute all t'
time, and as soon as ever they were ready, and
that was n't long after it were light, away they
goes towing t' two boats behind, and giving it
to her straight for t' Labrador. 'Skipper Life,'
Bill shouted, just after the anchor was up,
'if you sees Louis be sure and tell him to be
good and say his prayers, and when he is
ready, not to forget his uncles in Labrador and
come over and settle down peaceful like.'

"No, Doctor, Louis never got so much as a
match back, though he wrote and wrote about
it — and Louis were a good scholar, being well
learnt in France. All t' Government did was to
offer Captain Fordland, who fished t' big Jersey rooms across near Isle au Loup on Labrador, another hundred dollars to bring back
Skipper Bill with him in t' fall. T' captain told
his men that they could divide t' money

Portland Bill

if they liked to catch old Portland out of hours.

"I 'lows it was more t' fun of hunting than anything else that started 'em, though two hundred dollars cash meant a nice bit in them times. Soon there were half a dozen small crowds keeping an eye out for Bill. There were no wires or mail steamers to carry news them days, and it so happened that Bill fell right into t' trap. For Captain Fordland did a bit o' trade, and Bill, being out of flour, come along to buy a barrel. Half a dozen men soon had him and his boat as well. T' trouble was where to keep him till they went home in t' fall, which was a full two months anyhow.

"The crowd what took him got leave from Skipper Fordland to lock Bill up in t' top storey of t' old Jersey brick store on the Island; and 'em fixed it like sailors so that not even Bill should get away. They had to share t' expense of feeding and looking after he between 'em, and though they did n't give he none too much it took quite a bit of their wages — only a hundred dollars for the whole summer.

Labrador Days

"Bill had been there nearly six weeks and all hands were thinking of going home, when one day he told t' cook who brought up his food that he was fair dying of doing nothing, and could n't he give him some work. Being an old sailor, he set Bill to making bread bags, and for a few days he made a whole lot, and t' cook took it easy. All he gave Bill was some canvas, a pocket-knife, and some needles and thread. Bill, however, saved a lot of canvas out of them bags and made himself a long rope of it. Then he just worked on, waiting for a real dark night and an offshore wind, when he let hisself down through t' window, swam off to t' best fishing bully Captain Fordland had, and was out of sight before daylight.

"You may bet they was all mad, more especially t' captain, who swore that t' crowd would have to pay for his good boat. What they said and did to t' cook be scarcely fit for ears to hear. Anyhow, no one knowed where Bill had gone, and none of that crowd ever saw him again. He were n't very dear to memory either.

Portland Bill

"'T' next place us heard of him was on the West Coast. He brought with him an Eskimo wife he called Nancy, who was very good at doctoring. She could make poultices out of herbs and medicines out of t' woods, and she would charm toothache and warts and such like, and could stop bleeding by just tying green worsted round your left arm. She had a haddock's fin-bone that never touched any boat that she used to lend out for rheumatism. She did a lot o' good, they says, Doctor, and she made a nice bit of money, too, so that old Bill had an easy time. But he spent most of t' cash in liquor, and at last she would n't work any more for he and he got beating her. One day he come rowing down right into Port Warfield, with she tied up in t' bottom of t' boat, and a stone tied round her neck as well! It so happened that big Skipper Weymouth came alongside and seed her.

"'What be you going to do wi' she?' he asked, he not being afraid as most were. 'Why drown her, to be sure,' said Bill. 'I towed her behind t' boat for a mile a week ago come Sunday to drive t' devil out of her. But she ain't no good to me now, and so I reckon I'll get another.'

"The skipper saw that Bill had liquor in him and was quarrelsome, and feared that he'd just as likely as not upset t' boat — and drowned t' woman would be sure enough with that stone round her neck. So he says, 'Drown her! Not on this coast and lobsters just setting in. She'd spoil the catch all summer just to spite you.' Bill looked puzzled. 'You're right, sure enough, Skipper Alf. I'll have to do for she some other way' — and round he goes and rows her home again.

"The people, howsomever, was real afraid, and letters went up to the Government. No doubt Bill heard about it. But there were no place left now for him to go safely, so he just drank and drank where he was, all he could lay hands on; and when he could n't get no more I guess he must have gone mad. For he were found dead on t' floor of his house, with a great big knife he had for hunting deer in his hand.

Portland Bill

"Yes, his wife's alive to this day so far as us knows. Her son Bill found a box of old silver dollars, Spanish and French, buried under t' house Bill had on Labrador, the time he were trapped by Captain Fordland's men. They were mostly about a hundred years old. I saw many of them, but where they come from, or how he come by 'em, no one ever knew. We heard, however, that they helped poor Nancy to get back to her people again all right."

KAIACHOUOUK

THE brief summer of Northern Labrador had passed, and the Eskimos around the Hudson's Bay Post at Katatallik were busy preparing for the approaching winter. The season previous, according to the accurate notes of the Moravians, kept for over a hundred years, had been the worst on record; and now again, as the long, cold, icy grip of winter drew near, the prospect of supplies was menacingly poor. So the Innuits, that cheerful and resourceful little race of the North who wrest their living from so reluctant an environment, were putting forth all their energies in a "preparedness" from whose example many a civilized community might well have profited.

Their chief Kaiachououk, of upright character, and the courage born of simplicity, was a familiar figure at the Hudson's Bay Post where my friend Barlow was *facteur* for so many years. His acquaintance with the chieftain dated from an afternoon many years be-

Kaiachououk

fore, when he had first seen him, steering his large oomiavik, or flat-bottomed boat, up to the station, while his four lusty wives cheerily worked at the sweeps with his eldest son — an almost regal procession. It was on that same evening that he had told the *facteur*, after watching Mrs. Barlow prepare the evening meal, "Ananaudlualakuk" ("She is much too good for you"), and the frankness of his speech, far from seeming to disparage his host, endeared the speaker all the more to that hospitable and discerning person.

Kaiachououk possessed qualities which evoked the respect and admiration of all with whom he came in contact. Very noticeable among these was his affection for his family. To this day on the coast there is a story told of him and his youngest wife. He had been camping on their outside walrus-hunting station, and as was customary, he was sometimes away two or three days at a time, having to take refuge on one of the off-lying islands, if bad weather or the fickleness of fortune involved longer distances to travel than he was able to accomplish in a short winter's day. It was on his return from one of these temporary absences that he was greeted with the news that his youngest wife, Kajue, was very ill. One might have supposed that having so generous a complement of that nature, the news would not have afflicted him in the same degree as one less gifted. But exactly the reverse proved to be the case. Kaiachououk was completely prostrated; and when the girl died two days later, having failed to make any rally in spite of all her husband's generous presents to Angelok, he literally went out of his mind.

The Eskimo custom, still observed in the North, is to lay out the dead in all their clothing, but with no other covering, on the rocky summit of some projecting headland. The body thus placed on the surface of the rocks is walled in with tall, flat stones standing on end, long, narrow slits being left between them, so that air and light may freely circulate, and the spirit of the departed may come and go at will and keep watch on passing animals, whose spirits must serve the person in the spirit land just as, when embodied, they paid tribute to the needs and prowess of the dead. The top of the grave is also covered with large, flat slabs; and in a small separate cache of similar construction are stored all the personal belongings likely to be of use. The spirits of these latter are set free, either by having holes bored in them or some part of them broken or removed, so that thus being rendered useless to the living, they suffer what in the Eskimo mind corresponds to the death of inanimate objects.

Kaiachououk was so convinced of the reality of the spirit world, and so heart-broken at his utter inability to bring back to life the one he had loved so well, that now nothing would satisfy his mind but that in order to continue the communion which had been so sweet to him on earth, he should be treated exactly as his lost wife, and be immediately buried alongside her on some point of vantage.

At first his followers were inclined to treat his injunctions as mere vapourings, but they finally realized that the man was in deadly earnest, and were eventually compelled to comply with his wishes. The day being set, he was accordingly dressed in his finest garments, and, his dead wife being duly caparisoned and walled in in the customary manner, Kaiachou- ouk, laid out on the rock beside her, was treated in an exactly similar fashion. There was no apparent alteration of the chief's attitude of mind as they proceeded with the walling up, and the heavy slabs were already being laid over him when two of the largest happened to become lodged on his chest. For a short time he made no sign and offered no kind of resist- ance; but it was gradually forced upon him that this method of translation into other worlds was far from being as easy as he had been inclined to suppose. Consequently, before the cortège had broken up and his last friends departed, he was loudly appealing to them to return and release him.

He was never known afterwards to refer to the incident; but on the whole it had an excel- lent effect on the Innuits; and they realized, so far as their unimpressionable natures are ca- pable of doing, the strong domestic affection for his wife which was one of their chief's pre-eminent sources of greatness.

On this particular fall, when the last drama in Kaiachououk's life was played, when the northern lights sent their many-coloured banners floating over the heavens, and the stars looked so large and shining that it seemed one must surely touch them from the tops of the high hills, he was camping with his family and two or three others on a small ledge at the foot of the mighty Kiglapeit (shining top) Mountains, hunting walrus. This year the hunt was doubly important to them, and they delayed longer than was their wont. Here the great cape with which the spur ends marks the division of the whole trend of the land north from that which runs more directly south toward Katatallik. There the whole force of the south-going polar streams, focused on the ice, keeps open water long after all the rest of the coast is locked in the grim grip of winter. The walrus herds seem, in the evolution of ages, to have got an appreciation of this fact through their adamantine skulls. Therefore, from time immemorial, it has been chosen as a rendezvous of the Innuits in spring and fall. The chaos of ancient walrus bones which strews the stony beach reminds one of nothing so forcibly as the stacks of bleaching buffalo bones which disgrace the prairies.

On several occasions during the year previous, Kalleligak (the Capelin) had been guilty of the worst crime in the Eskimo calendar — on several occasions he had failed to extend that hospitality to strangers without which life on the coast is scarcely possible. It had been brought to Kaiachououk's notice, and he had lost no time in seeking out the man and taxing him with his remissness. A mixture of traits like the colours in a variegated skein of worsted formed the spectrum of Kalleligak's character; and selfishness, which fortunately is rarer among the Eskimos than among those in keener competition with civilization, was too often the prevailing colour. After the interview, at which he had promised to mend his ways, he apparently always lived in fear that sooner or later Kaiachououk would have him

Kaiachououk

punished, and even deprive him of some of his possessions. The obsession haunted him as the thought of the crime does the murderer, and at last impelled him to the act which, though it went unpunished by men, blasted the remainder of his days.

Among the others who camped around Kaiachououk's igloo this year was as usual the sub-chief Kalleligak. He had been more than usually successful in his hunt, and was able to face the prospect of the oncoming winter with optimism. On the other hand, his supposed enemy, Kaiachououk, had been singularly unfortunate, largely owing to the fact that his kayak had been left farther to the north. He showed no signs of either impatience or jealousy, however, and never by word or act gave evidence that he so much as remembered the rebuke he had been forced to administer to the sub-chief. Finally he dispatched his eldest sons, Bakshuak and Kommak, with a big team of dogs, to hurry down north and bring the belated and forgotten boat back with all speed.

Kalleligak, obsessed by his jealousy and

chagrin, was able from his camp to watch every movement of the chief's. He positively brooded so much over the incident that he came to believe that his life was in danger at Kaiachououk's hands. The next steps were easy, for he was favoured both by the innocence of his superior and the weather. Days are short in the late fall in the North, and darkness falls before work is finished.

In the late afternoon, two days after Bakshuak and Kommak's departure, while Kaiachououk was still out of his igloo and the darkness was rapidly coming on, Kalleligak stole inside and took the chief's gun. This he unloaded and then reloaded with two balls. Early next morning, before the dawn, he crept out, carrying his own and the stolen weapon, to watch his chance. Kaiachououk, emerging soon after from his snow house, turned his back on Kalleligak's igloo while he stooped to make a trifling repair on his own. Without a second's hesitation, Kalleligak seized Kaiachououk's own gun, and crawling and crouching up behind the five-foot snow ramparts which the

Kaiachououk

Eskimos invariably build around their winter houses, he fired two bullets through the unsuspecting man's back and body. The chief fell head foremost, having received two fatal wounds; but Kalleligak, throwing down one gun had instantly grabbed the other, in order if necessary to finish the deed before the mortally wounded man could tell who was responsible. But Kaiachououk never moved, and his enemy slunk inside, believing that he had been unobserved.

As fate would have it, Anatalik, another of the hunters, appeared at the entrance of his igloo just in time to see the smoking gun-barrel over the edge of the snow wall. Running to his fallen chief, he begged him to tell him what had occurred. The dying man had only strength left to whisper "Kiapevunga?" ("Who has killed me?"), and Anatalik could barely discern from his eye that he understood the answer, "Kalleligamut" ("It was Kalleligak who did it").

It was probably this, to us, unimportant item which caused a confession ever to be made.

Labrador Days

Kalleligak, now convinced that the spirit of his
dead chief knew he was the murderer, believed
it would haunt him without mercy, and that
his own life might be immediately forfeit unless he could appease it. He therefore at once
set about preparations for a funeral befitting
the dignity of the deceased; which, in the absence of Kaiachououk's eldest son, he himself
personally supervised. When all was over he
went to the igloo carrying gifts, and offered to
support the entire family till the sons should
be of an age to assume it. His overtures were
as unwelcome as they were importunate; but
the poor women were forced to listen in silence.
Helpless as they were, with their young men
away, they dared not anger the man, whose
character was only too well known. Kalleligak,
in order further to allay the anger of the spirit,
with all speed set out on the trail to meet the
dead man's returning sons, and apprize them
personally of his version of the story.

Bakshuak, the eldest, listened in silence
while Kalleligak first recounted the long list of
imaginary wrongs which he had suffered at the

Kaiachououk

hands of his father, then made his plea of self-defence, and lastly recited the hateful overtures which he had made to the helpless family, who were now, in spite of themselves, under very definite obligations to the murderer.

Angrily the lad repudiated any parleying. The family would far rather starve than be beholden to such infamy as was suggested. He was only a boy now, he declared, but he said fearlessly that if no one else killed him, he would do the deed himself as soon as he was big enough; and he raced on with his dogs, to reach home and comfort his poor mother. Had he but known it, he was really indebted for his life to the supposed wrath of his father's spirit and the restraining effect which it had on Kalleligak.

Eskimos never refer to painful events if they can help it. They go even farther than certain modern "scientists," for if a person who dies happens to have had the same name as one still living in the vicinity, the latter incontinently changes his. As a result, confusion not infrequently arises, for a man whom you have known all his life as "John" is "William" the next time you meet him. Thus they avoid the mention of the word the memory of which might bring pain to the relatives. Much less would they bring bad news to a white man.

They took good care, however, that the local Innuits should know that Kaiachououk was dead, hoping that they might give the great white man at the post the sad news of the loss of his friend. Barlow, as soon as he was certain of the main facts, at once dispatched messengers to summon to him Kalleligak, and Anatalik, who had seen the deed. The murderer had already expressed his willingness to surrender to the white man, and he at once packed up and accompanied the couriers back to Katatallik.

Meanwhile the news had also reached Ekkoulak, the sister of Kaiachououk, and her husband, Semijak, immediately summoned his council to discuss matters. All were agreed that the tribal custom must be observed. "A life for a life" was the only law they recognized, and the two elder sons of Semijak were selected to

Kaiachououk

carry the sentence into effect. Well armed and equipped, they started the very next morning for the North. The following day they walked into the Hudson's Bay Post to apprize the white man of their errand, so that there might be no suspicion of their blood-guiltiness, not knowing that by a strange whim of fortune Kalleligak and Anatalik were already there and were seated in one room while they were being received in another.

In the room with Kalleligak and Anatalik was Mr. Barlow's daughter, a little child of six, who was amusing herself with a picture book of the life of Christ. The little girl began to show the pictures to the two men, telling them the story in their own tongue as she went along. She at last came to the picture of Christ upon the Cross between the two thieves. Mr. Barlow in the adjoining room heard Kalleligak ask the child if she thought Jesus would forgive any one who had killed another man, to which the little one replied, "Why, yes, if he were really sorry and tried to be better."

The house of friends is neutral ground, and

to start a quarrel in the great white man's house would be about as likely as that we should begin one on the steps of the altar. Thus, when Kalleligak and Anatalik were summoned to dinner, both parties proceeded as if nothing unusual were in the air and all refreshed themselves at the same board.

Bidding them to keep the peace, Mr. Barlow made an effort to get to the bottom of the affair; but he found it very hard to know what to advise. The sister of Kaiachououk had begged and prayed her sons, now chosen as avengers, to have nothing to do with the slaying, saying, "It will only make more trouble. It will be Kalleligak's family who will suffer. They will surely starve to death." She had even sent a special messenger to the agent with an earnest plea that he would use all his influence to save her lads from the shedding of blood.

Having decided that the matter should be settled in open court and to abide by the decision of the great white man, all concerned now adjourned to the kitchen, and not for the first time that humble room was transformed into a court of justice. Kalleligak first gave his version of the story without the slightest attempt to conceal anything. He said he had lived in constant terror of what Kaiachououk might inflict upon him; and then, turning to the two men, who were fully armed with loaded guns, he said: —

"I know you have come to kill me. I shall never know good fortune again, anyhow. I have many skins and goods. With those I will pay for Kaiachououk. I can say no more."

As he ceased speaking, Semijak's eldest son burst out angrily: —

"Yes, we have come to kill you. Our law is a life for a life. We will not take any bribe."

But Oggak, the second avenger, thought differently: —

"We will hurt those who are not guilty. It would be different if he had no family. What offer does he make?"

"You know that Kalleligak is the second best hunter in the North," the agent spoke up. "And your mother, the wife of Semijak, has

145

also sent me a letter. She says nothing but evil will come from killing the head of another family. Cannot the spirit be satisfied in some other way?"

Mr. Barlow said he would go out and return when they had talked over the matter among themselves. He always felt great pity for these far-off outcasts of humanity. To kill another could only make matters worse. It was quite probable that even a blood feud would be started and more valuable lives be sacrificed. The struggle for existence was hard enough in any case, and if he suggested their taking the law into their own hands, there was no telling where it would end.

So it turned out that the matter was settled by simple word of mouth. That was absolutely sufficient for Kalleligak. If the avengers appointed by the tribe were satisfied, not only would the spirit of the murdered chief rest quietly, but the guilty one's life would be safe.

The agreement, duly drawn up by the agent, read as follows: —

Kaiachououk

"We will not kill you.
You are to pay —
Two white bears.
Twelve white foxes.
Three live dogs."
That was the value set on a really great
man's life. It makes one wonder at what rate
ours would be appraised in Eskimo land.

TWO CHRISTMASES

IT was Christmas Eve, and Malcolm McCrea, just back from the woods, was throwing down some frozen seal meat from the scaffold for his hungry dogs after their long day's hauling. Malcolm was only eighteen, and in winter still lived with his father in their home below the falls of Pike's River. However, now that he had been away for two summers in his uncle's schooner fishing "down North," his eyes were already turned to some long-untenanted fjords in the mouths of which the craft had anchored.

Pike's Falls was a lonely place, and the sound of a human voice calling to a dog team kept Malcolm standing with a fine forkful of meat in his hands long enough so greatly to tantalize the team below as to start a serious fight. This woke him from his reverie. "Ah, Ah!" he shouted, and, jumping down right into the middle of the fracas, soon had his dogs busy again with the frozen blocks which constituted their food for the day.

Two Christmases

"Is that you, Mr. Norman?" he exclaimed heartily. "Why, who would ever have thought of seeing you here, and alone, this evening of all days in t' year?" — as a middle-aged man jumped from an empty sledge and began unharnessing a half-starved-looking team. "Shall I give you a hand? They seem spun out."

"Better not touch 'em, I reckon," was the gruff answer. "They're a bit surly with strangers." And indeed already the animals were snarling and showing their teeth at the other dogs finishing their meal near by.

Malcolm, who at once proceeded to throw down a liberal allowance of seal meat for the newcomers' suppers, attributed the savage way in which their master whipped off his host's team from trying to get a second helping, to the weariness of a long journey. For to beat another man's dogs, especially with the long and heavy lash of our Northern whips, is a breach of the unwritten law of the Labrador.

It was not until he had shared the steaming supper prepared for Malcolm that the strings of the visitor's tongue began to be unloosed. For

149

it is not etiquette to ask a stranger's reasons for visiting a well-stocked house, in a country where the komatik trail is the only resource for the destitute.

"It's to t' post I'm bound. We be short of grub south. T' fishery have been bad this three years, and there's six of us now," he began. "There wasn't more than a couple of bakings of flour in t' barrel when I left. I could n't get no credit south at Deep-Water Creek; and so I just had to try north or starve."

"'T is a long bit yet to t' post," replied Malcolm. "There is t' Monkey to cross if you goes inside; and us allows it a good hundred miles to go round t' cape. It'll take you a week to haul a barrel of flour from there here."

Roderick, sitting back in his chair, was dejectedly surveying the comfortable-looking room. Malcolm caught his gaze, and realized what was passing in the poor fellow's mind.

"Draw up, draw up, and light your pipe, Mr. Norman," he interposed. "'T is only Home Rule tobacco, but it serves us down here."

Two Christmases

Eagerly enough Norman accepted the proffered plug, and then relapsed into a silence which Malcolm found it hard to break. So, excusing himself for a minute, he beckoned the old folk to come into their bedroom that they might talk over the situation in private.

"He has four youngsters, and I knows they be hard up," he began. "They has n't a chance where they are. T' neighbours blames Roderick for several little troubles which happened to t' southard, and t' traders won't advance more 'n he can pay for. If it was any one else, and to-morrow was n't Christmas, it would be just good fun to go down North with him and help haul back a barrel or so — that is, if they lets him have it."

"That 's not like you, Malcolm. You can't make a man good that way, any more 'n you can a dog by beatin' him," chimed in his old mother. "I guess you 'll go along with him, even to-morrow, if so be he wishes it."

"S'pose I will, Mother, but —"

"'Course you would," said his father proudly. "They 've never known a McCrea yet on this coast that would let even a dog starve. But there's a barrel of flour in our cellar which we can live without. Maybe it's t' kind of Christmas greeting t' poor fellow needs."

"If you says so, it's all right, Father," said Malcolm, "and, seeing it's a good hundred miles to Mr. Norman's house, I guess I'll go along, anyhow, in t' morning and let my beauties help them half-fed pups of his, or it'll be Old Christmas Day before his kids get a bite out of it."

Only the joy of the first tobacco for weeks was keeping the worn-out man from being fast asleep when Malcolm again took a chair beside him.

"I've got to make a round south to-morrow, Mr. Norman," he began, "and it would be a pity if you had to be going t' other way. Father says he has a barrel of flour in t' cellar you can have and pay for it when youse can. So if that'll suit, I'd like to give you a hand some part of t' way, especially as there'll be a few gallons of molasses to carry also if you'll take 'em."

Two Christmases

Gratitude is a rare grace. The lack of it was one of the costly defects in Roderick's character. No longer hungry, sitting before a good fire with a well-filled pipe, even the cunning which usually supplies the vacancy failed him; and Malcolm had to force himself to put down to exhaustion the ungracious way in which his real sacrifice was accepted.

In spite of hard work, they had only made thirty miles by sunset the next day, and, there being no shelter, they were obliged to camp early as light snow was falling. Yet it was a good Christmas night around the blazing fire with the special cheer the old mother had packed into the bread-boxes on their komatik. The following morning they did better, reaching the landwash of a big inlet forty miles farther south by noon. Here Malcolm had decided to turn back, for the remainder of the trail to Long Point lay practically over level ice. Just as they were saying good-bye, however, his quick eye detected something black moving out on the bay.

"A fox, Mr. Norman. Look! A fox! And a

black one too. You may be able to pay for that barrel of flour before t' day's out."

They were both good furriers, and their plans were soon laid. The dogs were quickly hitched up to stumps, and, glad of a rest, were easily made to lie down. Alas, the men had only Malcolm's gun; but it was arranged that he should go out and turn the fox, and Norman, hiding at the third corner of the triangle, should try and shoot it passing or lure it in range down wind.

Things went admirably. Malcolm by a long détour was able to turn the fox from far out without frightening it. Roderick, well hidden, and squeaking like a mouse, tolled it into easy range; and within an hour the two men held in their hands a skin worth at least four hundred dollars. It was agreed, at Roderick's suggestion, that he should carry it home, as he was nearer the fur-buyers, take the first offer over that sum, and then send the half due by the law of the woods to Malcolm north by the earliest mail-carrier.

Malcolm added as he said good-bye, "I

reckon maybe Father will want to let t' barrel go as good luck on t' bargain."

Summer came, and open water with it, but the half value of that skin never arrived. Later, in reply to Malcolm's enquiry by letter, a note came to say that it was being held for a better price in the fall; and with that he had to be content.

Winter followed summer, and when once again the "going was good," Malcolm, "running light" with his dogs, made the journey to Long Point easily in two days. Yes, the skin was sold, but the agent had not yet sent the cash. It had brought $430 and the half would come along as soon as ever Monsieur Baillot forwarded the notes. But the winter again went by and no notes, no letters, or other news ever reached Malcolm McCrea. Six years passed, and still they never came, and the McCreas supposed the debt was time-barred. Indeed, they had almost forgotten the whole incident.

Malcolm was still nominally at his father's house, but for three winters he had trapped on the Grand River, which flowed out into one of the bays he had discovered "down North." Here with the help of a hired man he had built up quite a fine little house, and made every preparation for that momentous life experience which usually comes early in life to every Labrador man. With characteristic caution he had waited for a good winter hunt to buy furnishings and traps. This had also given Nancy Grahame, who lived close to his home, time to get ready the needed linen and other requisites. "Clewing up" his salmon fishery in good time, Malcolm had cruised North in his own small sailboat, and till the first ice made had been very busy cutting wood, hauling food into the country for the winter tilts along his fur-path on the Grand River, completing his cellar, and safely storing his winter house supplies.

His first hunt being mostly for foxes along the landwash of the bay, he had waited until the snow came to tail his traps, judging that although it would take a week with his dogs to fetch his wife to their new home, he might safely chance that length of time away without losing anything which might be snared in the meanwhile. This was the third winter he had furred this path without interruption, and by all the custom of the coast no one would now interfere with his claim. So Malcolm started south at a stretch gallop with a light heart.

The two hundred and odd miles to the rendezvous at his father-in-law's winter home in the woods were covered with only two nights out, and that when the trails were as yet hardly broken and the young ice on the rivers would surely have delayed any man with less determination.

The wedding was in real Labrador style. Every one from far and near was present, quite without the formality of an invitation. It would, indeed, be an ill omen for the future if any one were omitted through the miscarriage of an invitation. So the danger is averted by the grapevine telegraph, which simply signals the event in sufficient time to make it a man's own fault if he is not present. Malcolm had many friends and there had been great preparations in Capelin Bay. Every scrap of room was needed to accommodate the guests, and at night hardly an inch of floor space but lodged some sleeping form wrapped in a four-point blanket, while the hardier ones with sleeping-bags contentedly crawled into them out in the snow, as their fashion is when nothing better offers.

The cooking had to be done in two large net-barking cauldrons over open fires under the trees; and as the fall deer hunt had been successful, and pork had not in those days assumed the present impossible prices, there were all kinds of joints, and no limit to proteids and carbohydrates. The great plum puddings which served for wedding cakes were pulled out of the same boiling froth, tightly wrapped in their cloth jackets, with long fish "pews" or forks. Unlimited spruce beer, brewed with molasses and fortified with "Old Jamaica," flowed from a large barrel during the two days that the celebration lasted.

At twenty below zero a slight increase in the calories consumed or even in the excess of alcohol over the normal two per cent of spruce beer leaves little trace on hardy folk; and when on the third morning, McCrea and his bride fared forth behind their splendid dog-team, every guest was gathered at the starting-point to "whoop up" the departing couple.

"'T is early I'll be starting in t' morning, Nancy, for it's nigh a fortnight since I tailed my traps, and there were good signs, too, by t' boiling brooks," said Malcolm the first evening they arrived home. "A fox following t' land-wash from t' rattle must surely take t' path there, for t' cliff fair shoulders him off t' land, and t' ice is n't fast more'n a foot or so from t' bluff. 'T would be a pity to lose a good skin, and us just starting in housekeeping."

"What's right's right, Malcolm," answered his wife, pouting just perceptibly. "Us must end our honeymoon with the journey down. I'll not be lonely, I reckon, getting t' house to rights." And she laughed gayly as she noticed the results of Malcolm's sincere but unique attempts at furnishing.

"It'll be a ration of pork I'll be needing

Labrador Days

boiled, and a bun or two for my nonny-bag. I can cover t' path in two days so be t' going's good; but there's nothing like being prepared."

"Get a few more splits, then, boy," she replied, "and I'll be cutting t' pork t' while." For she knew that Malcolm's estimate of the supply necessary for a possible delay was not the preparedness which would satisfy her ideas.

Days are short in November in the North, and the moon was still up to see Malcolm picking his way along the unmade trail which led to the spot where the sea ice joined the "ballicaters" or heaped-up shore ice. In the late fall this is the happy hunting-ground of foxes, for a much-needed dinner is often to be picked up in the shape of some enfeebled auk or other seabird, while even a dead shark or smaller fish may be discovered.

This was only a brief fall hunt. Malcolm had some fifty traps over ten miles of country, all of which he would take up the following month when the sea ice froze on permanently to the shore, re-tailing them along his real fur-path up the Grand River along the bank of which he had no less than three small shacks some thirty miles apart. Here he made his long winter hunt for sables, otters, and lynxes, using nearly three hundred traps.

It was with keen expectation and brisk step that he now strode along over the open; only the unwritten law of silence for a trapper on his path prevented his whistling as he went. When passing through the long belt of woods which marks the edge of the river delta, he found numerous windfalls blocking his narrow trail; but, keyed up as he was, he managed to get by them without so much as rustling a twig. "I'm fending for two now," he said to himself, and the very thought was sweet, lending zest to the matching of his capacities against those of the wild.

There was nothing in his first two traps. He had n't expected anything. They were only a sort of outliers in case something went wrong with those in the sure places. But now he was nearing the Narrows, and already his fence running from the steep bluff to the river edge was visible. But there was no fox in number three. The trap had not been sprung. The bait was as he had left it. "Maybe there'll be more to t' eastward," he thought, "though there were signs on this side of t' river." And, resetting the trap, he plodded along farther on his round.

Midday came. He had passed no less than fifteen of his best traps, and not only had no fox been found, but not one trap was sprung or one bait taken.

Malcolm stood meditatively scratching his head by trap twenty. "Something's wrong," he said to himself, — "but what? Better boil t' kettle and think it over. Perhaps better luck after lunch."

Unstringing his tomahawk, he started to find some dry wood with which to kindle a fire. None being close to the beach, he walked a few yards into the forest, and had just commenced on a tree when he noticed by the white scar that a branch had been broken quite recently from the very same trunk. "Wind and t' weight of t' silver thaw," he supposed, for there was no one living within fifty miles, and no other fur-path at that time, anyhow, in the bay. The northern komatik trail crossed twenty miles seaward, where the calm, wide expanse made the ice much safer in the early winter than near the swift current at the river mouth. But as he stooped to clear the trunk for his own axe, he noticed that, though disguised as a break, a cut had been first made to weaken the bough. "Some one's been here, that's sure," he said to himself. "Who can it be?" So much snow had fallen since Malcolm had gone after his wife that it was no easy matter to guess an answer — much less to read it from the trails around.

His frugal meal finished, he sat meditatively smoking his pipe by the glowing embers of his generous fire. But no light came to him. Practically no one lived near. The few who did were as honest as daylight. He had not an enemy on earth so far as he knew; and yet he realized now that the good condition of his traps, and especially his baits, after a fortnight of the blusterous Labrador fall weather needed accounting for. Well, anyhow, there was only one thing to do — go and finish his round, and when he got back he could talk the trouble over with his wife.

Slipping on his snow racquets and once more shouldering his nonny-bag, he strode off toward his next trap. It was new to him to suspect men. It was his business as a trapper to suspect Nature. It was, however, from this new viewpoint that he must approach his next task. For therein lies the intense interest of the trapper's life — every moment affords a keen problem. The gambler has the excitement of a possible big return, a sudden acquisition of gain. The trapper has all that, and the added satisfaction of knowing that it is his ability and not merely his luck which has won out.

At first sight there seemed nothing amiss with trap twenty-one. It had been tailed on the top of a specially felled tree. There it was still — a little mound of snow above the great expanse of whiteness, only recognizable because a trapper knows every inch of his path as a priest does his breviary. True, as the surface snow was only two days old, many marks could not be expected upon it. All the same, it struck Malcolm as odd that not a single fox-footing had he sighted since leaving home. "Something must have been cleaning 'em up," he reasoned. "There were two broods on Whale Island and one at least on t' Isle of Hope. That's some twenty all told — and ne'er a wolf or lynx track out to t' landward t' year." Musing to himself, he knelt down by the trap to examine it more closely. Lifting it up, he blew off the loose snow and inspected the stump carefully. No, nothing to indicate that it had been moved. If it had been, it must have been replaced with consummate care; for the rain had fallen once since Malcolm had tailed it, and the trap lay exactly in the icy trough, its handle and chain lying in the same groove. But the very fact suggested an idea. Possibly, if he cleared the snow there might be a frozen footmark in the hard surface beneath. Carefully, handful by handful, he removed over a foot of snow from around the bottom of the old tree, till he felt with his fingers the frozen crust. It took him over an hour's cold, tedious work, for he feared to use a mitten to protect his hand lest he should destroy the very traces of which he was in search. Though it froze his fingers and meant a long delay, it was well worth while, for he had undeniable evidence of a man's footmark, without any racquet, made since the rain previous to the last snowfall. It was probably at least a week old.

Again he examined the trap carefully. Not a hair, not a blood mark, not a sign to show that any fox had been in it. If it had been robbed, an expert had done it. There was another chance, however. Using his racquet as a spade, Malcolm was soon at work clearing the snow away right around the roots. The chain was a long one, and driven into one of the leaders was a steel fastener. It was as he expected. Not only had the chain been obviously gnawed, but there was considerable chafing of the bark as well. "He's been in it, sure enough, but the question is, Who's got t' skin?" Dark was coming on. There was no use going back; so, cutting down a few boughs and making a small lean-to under a big spruce, Malcolm kindled a blazing fire, "cooked the kettle," and turned in for the night.

Nancy had seen her husband as soon as he crossed the shoulder of the hill on his home-coming the third morning. To tell the truth, it was her first experience of being quite alone in the forest, and she had been doing but little "furnishing" after the first night. Now she was sure he had made a fine haul, and hurried out to meet him and hear the news. Malcolm, with the canniness of his kind, at once told her he had had no luck.

Now the actual amount of money lost may not have been great, but it had the irritating feature of being an unknown quantity and the additional vague risk of making all his winter work fruitless. It is useless to set traps if some one else is to follow around and rob them. So that night he told his wife the whole story. Discuss it as they would, there was no clue of any kind to follow; so like wise folk they decided to go on their way as if nothing had happened, keeping their mouths shut and their eyes and ears open.

No one visited their bay before Malcolm went on his first long fur round, which he did earlier than was his wont in order to be back in time for the first of the two winter mails. This trip he made a much better hunt, setting his traps as he went into the country. He took good care to make long marches, and even one day to double back on his tracks, making a long détour to see if he might not possibly pick up some unexpected signs of another man on *his* path. His, because, although there is no law on the subject, custom is law on Labrador, and the man who first finds a new trail for trapping has a conceded right of at least a mile in width for just as far as he cares to go.

The whole round was made in ten days, and, coming back with six sables, two otter, and a few mink and ermine, he was fortunate enough to reach home some hours before the southern mail team.

"What's t' news, Pat?" he asked, when at

Two Christmases

last supper was over, and the final pipe was being discussed by the fire.

"Nothing to boast of," was the answer. "T' same old story, with some a feast and with some a famine. They do say Roderick Norman's luck seems to have turned at last. T' Company gave he over four hundred dollars for a dark silver he got, and as much more, some say, for a batch o' reds and patches. 'T is more than good luck that half-breed must have had, for he has n't had a dozen traps to his name this five years."

Before he had finished speaking, Malcolm was watching him narrowly, wondering if some sprite had whispered abroad the robbing of his traps. But Pat was evidently unconscious of any possible connection between his news and his audience. As absolute silence was the only possible road ever to learning the truth, Pat left the next day on his journey north, not a whit the wiser for his night at the new homestead.

"It do sound strange, Nancy, don't it?" said her husband, after their guest had gone.

169

Labrador Days

"Roderick Norman can't have any grudge against me. Why, sure, it should be all t' other way." And he got up, stretched his splendid muscular limbs, and, picking up his axe, took out any excess of feeling there might be in his heart by a good two hours' work at the woodpile.

Meanwhile his mind had not been idle. Whoever it was that robbed his traps could not have come along the usual trail. The ice outside had not been safe for travelling. He certainly must have come out from the country. It had never occurred to Malcolm to spend time exploring the land which lay south of his fur-path. But now it seemed to him that he must at all costs set out the following morning and verify his suspicions if he were to retain his hope of a livelihood in that locality.

"I'm minded to try it right away, Nancy," said Malcolm. "If I could only get a good view from one of t' hilltops, I'd have no trouble, for there is still plenty of food in my tilts."

"But, Malcolm, 't is only two days till Christmas and this is our first together. Surely no one ever goes on the fur-path Christmas-time."

"That's just it, lass. No one is on t' path as ought to be, and I reckon for that very reason there be more chance of seeing those as ought not."

There was no escaping the logic of the Scotchman, and his wife acquiesced without further argument. He was well into the country before daylight next day.

It was a glorious morning, as away there in utter solitude the evergreen trees, the red-faced cliffs, the startling whiteness of the snow, and exquisite blue overhead fading into the purple distance of the winding valley met his keen view from a mountain-top. It was Labrador at its best — clear, dry, cold, and not a sound to break the absolute silence, even the trickling of the rapids and the splashing of distant falls being muffled by their heavy cloaks of ice.

Suddenly Malcolm's face grew rigid and his eyes unconsciously fixed themselves on a moving object — a tiny whiff of blue smoke was curling up from the woods on the other side of the valley. Gentle though he was, his big muscles set and his jaw tightened as the idea of revenge flashed across his mind.

A man does not learn to outwit successfully the keen senses of the denizens of the woods without finding it easy to solve a problem such as the one which Malcolm now faced. For all that, he decided not to approach too close till dark what he was now sure was a hut, for the way the smoke rose was quite unlike that from an open fire. Having, therefore, plenty of time, he made a long and cautious détour till he had at last completely encircled the spot. There were the marks of one pair of snow racquets only on the snow. The trail was possibly three days old. No snow had fallen for several days. "Reckon he is taking a good spell with that catch of his."

This much he knew. He knew the stranger was in or close to the tilt. He was not trapping, though he had been inside the circle for several days, and he had no dogs.

As it fell dark, Malcolm fully expected to see

Two Christmases

a light in the hut, but not a twinkle showed through the single-pane window light, which he had located from his hiding-place.

Now he was crawling nearer. There was no chance of his being seen, as the moon had not yet risen and it was very dark among the trees. A light wind had risen, rustling the firs and spruces above his head. The fire worried him. Why had it almost died out? Heaven knows it was cold enough to need one, for with all his warm blood Malcolm himself was shivering. What could it mean?

Suddenly he heard some one move inside. Then came the noise of sticks hitting a tin camp-stove and a sudden blaze flared up, burnt for a minute or two, and apparently went out again. Whoever it was must be ill, or hurt. He had no big billets or he would n't be firing with twigs.

It could not do any harm now to enter, and Malcolm strode noisily to the door and peered inside.

A man's weak voice greeted him. "Who's there? For God's sake, come in."

173

Labrador Days

"My name's Malcolm McCrea. Where's your light?"

"Haven't got one. I've no candle either," came the answer. "Had an accident three days ago with my gun, and nearly blew my foot off. My leg's swelled up something wonderful."

The voice, feeble almost to a whisper, conveyed no information as to the man's identity, except that the Scotchman's quick ear detected that there was resentment somehow mixed with satisfaction that a rescuer had come.

"I've a drop of kerosene in my nonny-bag," was all Malcolm said, "but it's scarce, and I 'low I'll cut up some wood and get t' fire going before lighting up. You lie quiet for a minute or two and I'll get you a drop of tea."

"Lie quiet!" snarled the other. "I've lain quiet for three days, and expected to stay till doomsday. It's no virtue keeps me lying quiet. I had no business to be here, anyhow, seeing there was no need of it."

"Well, do as you please," answered McCrea. And without much delay he soon had a roaring fire in the camp-stove which turned

Two Christmases

the chimney red-hot and made it possible to see dimly stretched out on a bed of fir boughs the long, thin form of a man whose drawn, unshaven face showed that he was suffering much pain. His right foot was swaddled in an ominously stained bundle of rags — evidently some torn-up garment.

Methodically lighting the bit of wick which he had placed in the kerosene bottle, Malcolm knelt down by the side of the injured man and, peering into the semi-darkness of the gloomy corner, found himself looking right into the eyes of Roderick Norman.

Having made some hot tea and shared it with the sick man, he offered him part of the pork and hard biscuit, all that he had with him for his own supper. But Roderick was too feeble to touch more than a bit of it soaked in hot tea, and that seemed a small strength-giver for such a time of need.

"If you'd a bit o' wire or line, I'd tail a snare for a rabbit when the moon rises and try if we could n't get a drop o' hot stew to help out. But I have n't a bit in my bag."

Labrador Days

"There's a couple o' traps," growled the sick man, and then stopped suddenly, shutting his jaws with a snap.

Malcolm looked around, but was unable to see any signs of them. "Where did you say they were?" he enquired; but no response came from the bunk.

McCrea finished his supper, lit his pipe, and suggested trying to wash the wounded foot. But fearing to start the bleeding again, they decided to leave it till morning.

"Where are those traps you spoke of, sir? The moon is beginning to show and I'll be needing to get 'em put out, if we're to have any chance." But still the other man made no answer. Malcolm went up close to the bed and knelt down by him again. "Mr. Norman," he said, "we're in a bad hole here. We're fifty miles from help, anyhow. We've no dogs and only one of us can walk. Moreover, there's almost no food. If you've got any traps, why not tell me where they are. I'm not going to steal 'em."

Roderick Norman opened his eyes and

Two Christmases

looked at him. The dim rays of the little wick in the kerosene bottle gave scarcely enough light to show the ordinary eye where the lamp itself was. But when their glances met, it was enough to show Roderick that it was no longer a child with whom he was dealing. For a second neither spoke, then Malcolm, putting his hand on the man's shoulder, gripped it perhaps more roughly than he intended. "The traps," he repeated.

Roderick winced. He saw that his secret was out. He was at the Scotchman's mercy, and he knew it. "They're stowed in t' hollow of t' old trunk, fifty yards back of t' tilt, damn you," he snarled, and tried to roll over, groaning bitterly with pain of both body and soul.

The pity of it appealed straight to Malcolm's generous heart, and his grip relaxed instantly. He strove to make the other more comfortable, moving him gently in his great arms.

"Forget it, Mr. Norman," he said. "No one shall ever know unless you tell 'em. I'll give you my word for that."

The sick man said nothing. His deep breathing, painfully drawn, was, however, enough in that dead silence to warn Malcolm of the struggle going on so close to him — a struggle so much more momentous than one of tooth and claw. He slipped his hand into that of the other and held it gently.

"You're very hot, sir," he remarked, just for something to say. "Shall I get you some cold water?"

But still there was no answer. Evidently the man's mind was engrossed with other thoughts. A long pause followed.

"Mr. Norman, for God's sake, forget it. No one's been hurt but yourself. If there's been any wrong, it's all forgiven and forgotten long ago. Let's just begin again. Remember 't is Christmas Eve night."

Still there was no reply, but McCrea's intuition saved him from the mistake of saying more. The stillness became uncanny. Then an almost imperceptible pressure of the sick man's hand sent a thrill vibrating through the Scotchman's soul. Yes, and he had himself returned the pressure before he knew it. A shiver passed over the sick man's frame and the silence was broken by a sob.

With an innate sense of fellow-feeling, Malcolm laid down the other's hand, rose, and went out without a word. The night was perfect with the glorious light of the waning moon. His mind was at once made up. He would be home by daylight and back again with his dogs by midday, with stimulants and blankets, and could have Roderick in Nancy's skilled hands before night.

Noiselessly opening the door, he filled the stove once more, piled up spare billets close to the bedside, laid out what food was left, placed his kettle full of water on the ground within reach of the sick man, and, just whispering, "I'll be back soon, sir," disappeared into the night.

How fast he sped only the stars and moon shall say. But joy lent him wings which brought him home before daylight. His faithful dogs, keeping their watch and ward out in the snow around his house, first brought the news to Nancy that her man was back so soon.

A few minutes served to explain how matters stood, and in a few more everything was ready. The coach-box was strapped on the komatik. The bearskin rug and a feather bed were lashed inside it, with all the restoratives loving care could think of, and with the music of the wild barking of the dogs echoing from the mountain and valley, the sledge went whirling back over the crisp snow — the team no less excited than Malcolm himself at this unexpected call for their services.

Everything was silent as once more they approached the scene of trouble. The dogs, panting and tired, having had no spell since they started, no longer broke the stillness with their barking. Malcolm hitched them up a hundred yards or so from the tilt, preferring to approach it on foot. He had long ago noticed that no smoke was coming from the funnel and it made his heart sink, for even in the woods the cold was intense.

Malcolm always says that he knew the meaning of it before he opened the door. Roderick Norman had gone to spend his first Christmas in happier hunting-grounds.

THE LEADING LIGHT

It was getting late in the year. The steep cliffs that everywhere flank the sides of the great bay were already hoary with snow. The big ponds were all "fast," and the fall deer hunt which follows the fishery was over. Most of the boats were hauled up, well out of reach of the "ballicater" ice. The stage fronts had been taken down till the next spring, to save them from being torn to pieces by the rising and falling floe. Everywhere "young slob," as we call the endless round pans growing from the centre and covering the sea like the scales of a salmon, was making. But the people at the head of the bay were still waiting for those necessities of life, such as flour, molasses, and pork, which have to be imported as they are unable to provide them for themselves, and for which they must wait till the summer's voyage has been sent to market and sold to pay for them.

Labrador Days

The responsibility of getting these supplies to them rested heavily on the shoulders of my good friend John Bourne, the only trader in the district. Women, children, whole families, were looking to him for those "things" which if he failed to furnish would mean such woeful consequences that he could not face the winter without at least a serious attempt to provide them.

In the harbour lay his schooner, a saucy little craft which he had purchased only a short while before. He knew her sea qualities; and as the ship tugged at her chains, moving to and fro on the swell, she kept a fine "swatch" of open water round her. Like some tethered animal, she seemed to be begging him to give her another run before Jack Frost gripped her in his chilly arms for months to come. The fact that he was a married man with hostages to fortune round his knees might have justified his conscience in not tempting the open sea at a time when frozen sheets and blocks choked with ice made it an open question if even a youngster ought to take the chances. But it

The Leading Light

happened that his "better half," like himself,
had that "right stuff" in her which thinks of
itself last, and her permission for the venture
was never in question.

So Trader Bourne, being, like all our men, a
sailor first and a landsman after, with his crew
of the mate and a boy, and the handicap of a
passenger, put to sea one fine afternoon in late
November, his vessel loaded with good things
for his necessitous friends "up along." He was
encouraged by a light breeze which, though
blowing out of the bay and there ahead for
him, gave smooth water and a clear sky.

To those who would have persuaded him to
linger for a fair wind he had cheerfully count-
ered that the schooner had "two sides," meaning that she could hold her own in adversity,
and could claw well to windward; besides,
" 't will help to hold the Northern slob back"
— that threatening spectre of our winters.

When darkness fell, however, very little
progress had been made. The wind kept shift-
ing against the schooner, and all hands could
still make out the distant lights of home twin-

kling like tiny stars, apparently not more than a couple of miles under their lee.

"Shall us 'hard up,' and try it again at day' light?" suggested the mate. "If anything happens 't is a poor time of year to be out all night in a small craft."

But the skipper only shrugged his shoulders, aware that the mate was never a "snapper" seaman, being too much interested in gardens for his liking.

"It's only a mile or two to Beach Rock Cove. We'll make it on the next tack if the wind holds. 'T is a long leg and a short one, and we'll have a good chance then to make the Boiling Brooks to-morrow."

"Lee oh!" and, putting the helm up, the Leading Light was soon racing off into the increasing darkness towards the cliffs away on the opposite side of the bay.

The wind freshened as the evening advanced — the usual experience of our late fall nights. An hour went by, and as the wind was still rising, the flying jib was taken in. After this the captain sent the crew below for a

The Leading Light

"mug o' tea" while he took the first trick at the wheel.

Still the wind rose. The sea too was beginning to make, and the little craft started to fall to leeward too much to please the skipper. The men were again called, and together they reset all the head canvas. The Leading Light now answered better to her helm, and, heading up a point, reached well into the bay.

"Smooth water again before dawn," said the skipper in his endeavour to cheer the despondent mate, when once more they had gone aft. "Looks like clearing overhead. I reckon she'll be well along by daylight."

But the mate seemed "stun," and only grunted in return.

"You go down and finish supper, and then you can give me a spell at the wheel while I get my pipe lighted," continued the captain. Thereupon the other, nothing loath to have something to keep his mind diverted, was soon below, searching for consolation in a steaming mug, but failing to find it, in spite of the welcome contrast between the cosy warm cabin,

185

and the darkness and driving spume on deck,
lacking as he did, alas, the sea genius of our
race.

"Watch on deck!" at length called Bourne;
and a few minutes later, having entrusted the
helm to the mate, he was lighting his pipe at
the cabin fire. All of a sudden down, down,
down went the lee floor of the cabin, and up,
up, up went the weather, till it felt as if the
little ship were really going over.

"What's up?" the skipper fairly yelled
through the companion, as clinging and struggling his utmost he forced his way on deck,
as soon as the vessel righted herself enough to
make it possible. "Hard down! Hard down!
Let her come up! Ease her! Ease her!" — and
whether the puff of wind slackened or the
mate lost hold of the wheel, he never has been
able to tell, but she righted enough for a moment to let him get on the deck and rush
forward to slack up the fore-sheet, bawling
meanwhile through the darkness to the mate
to keep her head up, as he himself tore and
tugged at the rope.

The Leading Light

The schooner, evidently well off the wind, yet with all her sheets hauled tight and clewed down, was literally flying ahead, but trying to dive right through the ponderous seas, instead of skimming over and laughing at them, as the captain well knew she ought to do. There was n't a second to lose pondering the problem as to why she would not come up and save herself. Difficult and dangerous as it was in the pitch dark with the deck slippery with ice, and the dizzy angle at which it stood, the only certain way to save the situation was to let go that sheet. Frantically he struggled with the rope, firmly clinched though it was round its cleats with the ice that had made upon it. Knowing how sensitive the vessel was and that she would answer to a half-spoke turn of the wheel, and utterly at a loss to understand her present stubbornness, he still kept calling to the helmsman, "Hard down! Hard down!" — only to receive again the growling answer, "Hard down it is. She's been hard down this long time."

It was all no good. Up, up came the weather

rail under the terrific pressure of the wind. The fore-sheet was now already well under water, cleat and all, and the captain had just time to dash for the bulwark and hold on for dear life, when over went the stout little craft, sails, masts, and rigging, all disappearing beneath the waves. It seemed as if a minute more and she must surely vanish altogether, and all hands be lost almost within sight of their own homes.

Tumultuous thoughts flooded the captain's mind as for one second he clung to the rail. Vain regrets were followed like lightning by a momentary resignation to fate. In the minds of most men hope would undoubtedly have perished right there. But Captain Bourne was made of better stuff. "Nil desperandum" is the Englishman's soul; and soon he found himself crawling carefully hand over hand towards the after end of the vessel. Suddenly in the darkness he bumped into something soft and warm lying out on the quarter. It proved to be his passenger, resigned and mute, with no suggestion to offer and no spirit to do more than lie and perish miserably.

The Leading Light

Still climbing along he could not help marking the absence of the mate and the boy from the rail, which standing out alone against the sky-line was occasionally visible. Doubtless they must have been washed overboard when the vessel turned turtle. There was some heavy ballast in the schooner besides the barrels of flour and other supplies in her hold. Her deck also was loaded with freight, and alas, the ship's boat was lashed down to the deck with strong gripes beneath a lot of it. Moreover, it was on the starboard side, and away down under water anyhow. Though every moment he was expecting the Leading Light to make her last long dive, his courage never for a second deserted him.

He remembered that there was a new boat on the counter aft which he was carrying with him for one of his dealers. She was not lashed either, except that her painter was fast to a stanchion. It was just possible that she might still be afloat, riding to the schooner as a sea anchor. Still clinging to the rail he peered and peered through the darkness, only to see the

great white mainsail now and again gleam
ghostlike in the dim light when the super-
incumbent water foamed over it, as the Leading Light wallowed in the sullen seas. Then
something dark rose against the sky away out
beyond the peak end of the gaff — something
black looming up on the crest of a mighty
comber. An uncanny feeling crept over him.
Yet what else could it be but the boat? But
what could that boat be doing out there? Fas-
cinated, he kept glaring out in that direction.
Yes, surely, there it flashed again across the
sky-line. This time he was satisfied that it was
the boat, and that she was afloat and partly
protected by the breakwater formed by the
schooner's hull. She was riding splendidly. In
an instant he recalled that he had given her a
new long painter; and that somehow she must
have been thrown clear when the ship turned
over. Anyhow, she was his only chance for life.
Get her he must, and get her at once. Every
second spelt less chance of success. Any moment she might break adrift or be dragged
down by the sinking schooner. And then came

the horrible memory that she too had been stowed on the lee side, and her painter also was under the mainsail and fastened now several feet below the surface. Even the sail itself was under water, and the sea breaking in big rushes over it with every comber that came along.

To get the boat was surely impossible. It only added to the horror of the plight to perish there miserably of cold, thinking of home and of the loved ones peacefully asleep so near, while the way to them and safety lay only a few fathoms distant — torturing him by its very nearness. For every now and then driving hard to the end of her tether she would rush forward on a sea and appear to be coming within his reach, only to mock him by drifting away once more, like some relentless lady-love playing with his very heartstrings. The rope under the sunken mainsail prevented her from quite reaching him, and each time that she seemed coming to his arms, she again darted beyond his grasp.

Whatever could be done must be done at

once. Even now he realized that the cold and wet were robbing him of his store of strength. Could he possibly get out to where the boat was? There might be one way, but there could be only one, and even that appeared a desperate and utterly futile venture. It was to find a footing somehow, to let go his vise-like grip of the rail, and leap out into the darkness across the black and fathomless gulf of water surging up between the hull and the vessel's main boom in the hope of landing in the belly of the sail; to be able to keep his balance and walk out breast high through the rushing water into the blackness beyond till he should reach the gaff; and so, clinging there, perchance catch the boat's painter as she ran in on a rebounding sea. There would be nothing to hold on to. The ever swirling water would upset a man walking in daylight on a level quayside. He would have nothing but a sunken, bellying piece of canvas to support him — a piece only, for the little leach rope leading from the clew to the peak marked a sharp edge which would spell the dividing line between life and death.

The Leading Light

He had known men of courage; he had read of what Englishmen had done. But he had never suspected that in his own English blood could lie dormant that which makes heroes at all times. A hastily breathed prayer — his mind made up, letting go of the weather rail he commenced to lower himself to the wheel, hoping to get a footing there for the momentous spring that would in all probability land him in eternity. But even as he climbed a little farther aft to reach down to it, he found himself actually straddling the bodies of the missing mate and boy, who were cowering under the rail, supported by their feet against the steering-gear boxing.

Like a thunderclap the whole cause of the disaster burst upon his mind. The mate's feet planked against the spokes of the wheel suggested it. The helm was not hard down at all, and never had been. It was hard up all the time. He remembered, now that it was too late, that the mate had always steered hitherto with a tiller; that a wheel turns exactly the opposite way to the tiller; and that with every sail hauled tight, and the helm held hard over, the loyal little craft had been as literally murdered as if she had been torpedoed, and also their lives jeopardized through this man's folly. What was the good of him even now? There he lay like a log, as dumb as the man whom he had left clinging to the taffrail.

"What's to be done now?" he shouted, trying in vain to rouse the prostrate figure with his foot. "Rouse up! Rouse up, you fool!" he roared. "Are you going to die like a coward?" And letting himself down, he put his face close to that of the man who by his stupidity had brought them all to this terrible plight. But both the mate and boy seemed paralyzed. Not a word, not a moan could he get out of them. The help which they would have been was denied him. Once more he realized that if any one was to be saved, he and he alone must accomplish it. A momentary rest between two waves decided him. There was one half-second of trying to get his balance as he stood up, then came the plunge into the wild abyss, and he found himself floundering in the belly of the sail, struggling to keep his footing, but up to his waist in water. With a fierce sense of triumph that he was safely past the first danger, the yawning gulf between the rail and boom, he threw every grain of his remaining strength into the desperate task before him, and pushed out for the gaff that was lying on the surface of the sea, thirty feet away in the darkness. Even as he started a surging wave washed him off his feet, and again he found himself hopelessly wallowing in the water, but still in the great cauldron formed by the canvas.

How any human being could walk even the length of the sail under such circumstances he does not know any more than I do. But the impossible was accomplished, and somehow he was clinging at last like a limpet to the very end of the gaff, his legs already dangling over the fatal edge, and with nothing to keep him from the clutch of death beyond it but his grip of the floating spar. To this he must cling until the mocking boat should again come taut on the line and possibly run within his reach.

The next second out of the darkness what seemed to the man in the sail a mountain of blackness rushed hissing at him from the chaos beyond, actually swept across him into the belly of the sail, and tore him from his rapidly weakening hold of the spar. With the energy of despair his hands went up and caught something, probably a bight in the now slackened painter. In a trice he was gripping the rail, and a second later he was safely inside the boat, and standing shaking himself like some great Newfoundland dog.

Even now a seemingly insuperable difficulty loomed ahead. He had no knife and was unable to let go the rope. Would he be able to take his comrades aboard, and would the schooner keep afloat and form a breastwork against the sea, or would it sink and, after all his battle, drag the boat and him down with it to perdition?

Philosophizing is no help at such a time. He would try for the other men. To leave them was unthinkable. Once more fortune was on his side. The oars were still in the boat, lashed

The Leading Light

firmly to the thwarts — a plan upon which he had always insisted. Watching his chance, and skilfully manœuvring, he succeeded in approaching the schooner stern first, when the cable just allowed him to touch the perpendicular deck. His shouts to the others had now quite a different ring. His words were commands, leaving no initiative to them. They realized also that their one and only chance for life lay in that boat; and returning hope lent them the courage which they had hitherto lacked. After a delay which seemed hours to the anxious captain at such a time, with skilful handling he had got all three aboard.

Once more he was face to face with the problem of the relentless rope, but again fortune proved to be on his side. It was the passenger, the useless, burdensome passenger, who now held the key to the situation. He had sensed the danger in a moment, and instantly handed the skipper a large clasp-knife. With it to free the boat from the wreck was but the work of a moment.

Labrador Days

True, their position in a small open "rodney" in the middle of a dark, rough night in the North Atlantic was not exactly enviable, especially as the biting winter wind was freezing their clothing solid, and steadily sapping their small stock of remaining vitality.

Yet these men felt that they had crossed a gulf almost as wide as that between Dives and Lazarus. If they could live, they knew that the boat could, for the ice would not clog her enough to sink her before daylight, and as for the sea — well, as with the schooner, it was only a matter of handling their craft till the light came.

Meanwhile, though they did not then know it, they had drifted a very considerable way towards their own homes, so that, rowing in turn and constantly bailing out their boat they at length made the shore at the little village of Wild Bight, only a few miles away from their own. The good folk at once kindled fires, and bathed and chafed the half-frozen limbs and chilled bodies of the exhausted crew.

The Leading Light

Now the one anxiety of all hands was to get home as quickly as possible for fear that some rumor of the disaster in the form of wreckage from the schooner might carry to their loved ones news of the accident, and lead them to be terrified over their apparent deaths. As soon as possible after dawn of day, the skipper started for home, having borrowed a small rodney, and the wind still keeping in the same quarter. To his intense surprise a large trap-boat manned by several men, seeing his little boat, hailed him loudly, and when on drawing near it was discovered who they were, proceeded to congratulate him heartily on his escape. Already the very thing that he had dreaded might happen must surely have occurred.

"How on earth did you know so soon?" he enquired, annoyed.

"As we came along before t' wind we saw what us took to be a dead whale. But her turned out to be a schooner upside down. We made out she were t' Leading Light, and feared you must all have been drowned, as there was no sign of any one on her upturned keel. So we were hurrying to your house to find out t' truth."

"Don't say a word about it, boys," said the skipper. "One of you take this skiff and row her back to Wild Bight, while I go with the others and try and tow in the wreck before the wind shifts. But be sure not to say anything about the business at home."

The wind still held fair, and by the aid of a stout line they were able, after again finding the vessel, to tow her into their own harbour and away to the very bottom of the Bight, where they stranded her at high water on the tiny beach under the high crags which shoulder out the ocean. By a clever system of pulleys and blocks from the trunks of trees in the clefts of the cliff she was hauled upright, and held while the water fell. Then the Leading Light was pumped out and refloated on the following tide. On examination, she was pronounced uninjured by her untimely adventure.

I owe it to John Bourne to say that the messenger forbidden to tell of the terrible ex-

The Leading Light

perience told it to his own wife, and she told it
— well, anyhow, the skipper's wife had heard
of it before the Leading Light once more lay
at anchor at her owner's wharf. Courage in a
moment of danger, or to preserve life, is one
thing. The courage that faces odds when the
circumstances are prosaic and the decision
deferred is a rarer quality. It was a real piece
of courage which gave the little schooner
another chance that fall to retrieve her repu-
tation. She was permitted to deliver the goods
against all odds, and what is more the captain's wife kissed him good-bye with a brave
face when once again he let the foresail draw,
and the Leading Light stood out to sea on her
second and successful venture.

There is no doubt that when she went to
bed in the ice that winter, she carried with her
the good wishes and grateful thanks of many
poor and lonely souls; and some have said that
when they were walking round the head of the
cove in which it was the habit of the little
craft to hibernate, strange sounds like that of
a purring cat were ofttimes wafted shoreward.

Labrador Days

"It is only the wind in her rigging," the skeptical explained; but a suspicion still lurks in some of our minds that the Eskimo are not so far from the truth in conceding souls to inanimate objects.

THE RED ISLAND SHOALS

THE house was fairly shaking in the gale, and any one but Uncle Rube, who had lived in it since he put it there forty years before, would have been expecting things to happen. But the old man sat dozing in his chair beside the crackling stove, and the circling rings of smoke rising over his snow-white head were the only signs of life about him. The only other occupant of the house was a little girl whom Uncle Rube had taken for "company," the year that his wife left him. The coast knew that his only lad had been lost aboard some sealer many years ago. The little girl was lying stretched out on the wooden settle close beside him. Twice already in the dim light of the tiny window, now well covered with snow outside and frost within, I had mistaken her towsly golden curls for a hearth-brush, she lay so still.

At length, as the cottage gave a more violent lurch than usual, even my book failed to keep my mind at rest.

"Aren't you afraid the house is going to blow away, Uncle Rube? You remember that our church blew into the harbor, pews and floor as well as walls and roof. You could see the pews at low water till the ice took them away."

Crack! Crack! Crack!

"No fear of she, Doctor. She's held on this forty years, and I reckon she won't bring her anchors home till I does myself."

"Never to go again till the old man died," I hummed.

Something, however, seemed to have roused up Uncle Rube. For, carefully laying his pipe in its place on the shelf, he went to the door, opening it enough to allow him to peer out through the crack. Unfortunately another eddying gust struck the house at that very moment, tore the door from his grasp, and by sweeping in and taking the fortress from within, very nearly gave it its *coup de grace*. In the momentary lull that followed we man-

The Red Island Shoals

aged to shut the door, and to barricade it from inside.

The child was astir before we got back to the genial warmth of the stove. Crack! Crack! Crack! went the little dwelling again, as a more than usually fierce blast of the hurricane, strengthened by the furiously driving snow, hit it like another hammer of Thor. Crack! Crack! The house seemed to swing like a pendulum before it came to rest again. I could see that the old man was uneasy.

"What is it, Uncle Rube? What is it?" the little girl cried out petulantly.

"Why, nothing, little one, nothing. Only 't is as well to take a peek out on times. There's no knowing when there might be some one astray through this kind of weather. 'T is no hurt to make sure, is it?"

She was a pale-faced little thing, with the lustrous eyes and delicate skin that often so pathetically array the prospective victims of the White Man's Curse. She had been a tiny, unwanted item in a large family of twelve with which "Providence had blessed" a struggling friend and neighbor. The arrival of the last had robbed him of his only help. "Daddy gived me to Uncle Rube," was her only explanation of her being there.

"'T is cold, though," she answered. "It made me dream that you were on the old island again, and I was with you, and then the house shook so that it woke me up."

For answer he went to an old and well-worn seaman's chest which served ordinarily for an additional seat. The reverent care with which he turned over the contents would have honored a priest before the sanctuary. But eventually he returned with a really beautiful shawl which he tenderly wrapped around the child, and sitting down laid her head upon his shoulder. In this position she was almost immediately asleep again, and, fearing to wake her, I had forborne to break the silence. Indeed, I was far enough away from ice and snow and blizzards for the moment — the Indian shawl having carried me home to England, and the old camphor trunk which my own mother, herself born in India, had taught us boys to

The Red Island Shoals

reverence as the old man did his, filled as ours was with specimens of weird patterns and exquisite workmanship.

Uncle Rube had been watching my eyes fixed on the rich mantle that contrasted so strangely with every other surrounding.

"I brought it from India when I used to go overseas. I keeps it because my Mary loved it so, though she 'lowed it was too rich for t' likes o' her to wear it much. But I guess it'll last now. 'T is t' last bit o' finery left," he smiled, "and 't is most time to be hauling that down. For I reckons Nellie won't last out to need it long. Eh, Doctor?" And for a moment a tear sparkled in his merry old eyes, as he peered from under his heavy white eyebrows.

"You can always trust me to find a good home for Nellie, Uncle Rube," I answered. "I've forty like her now, and one more won't sink the ship. But you know that better than I can tell you." And suddenly it flashed over me that Uncle Rube's unexpected visit to our Children's Home must had have some relation to the curly head on his shoulder. The tear fell on his tanned cheek, and he looked away and coughed. But he said nothing.

"What was the old island that Nellie was talking about?" I broke in to relieve the situation. "It sounded as if you had been playing Robinson Crusoe some time," I added, "and have spun her yarns that you won't tell me." For the hope that here might be something which would fill in the time during which it was plain that Jack Frost intended to keep me prisoner in this bookless cabin, suddenly dawned upon me.

"Island?" he smiled, after a brief pause. "Island? Oh! that was forty years ago, when us lost t' old Manxman on t' Red Island Shoals." And the *wanderlust* of Uncle Rube's British blood, stirred by this leap back over the passing years, made him once more a bouncing, devil-may-care sailor lad. The sign of tears had vanished from his cheeks as he rose, and, gently laying the little figure in her old corner on the settle, leisurely lit his pipe. Like that of Nathaniel Hawthorne's Feather-

The Red Island Shoals

top it seemed to send renewed youth through his veins with every puff he drew. Knowing that he was trying to think, and fearing to distract his mind, I again kept a discreet silence. At last, just as if he saw the scene again, his eyes closed and his splendid shock of long white hair was once more thrown back into its accustomed place in the rocking-chair.

"It was n't a fair deal, Doctor. Not a fair deal. We was sailors in those days, just as much as them is in they old tin kettles that rattles up and down t' Straits now, for all they big size and they gold braid. T' Manxman would n't have come by her end as she did if stout arms and good seamen could 'a' saved her. Murdered she was, Doctor, murdered by this same Jack Frost what's trying to blow us out o' house and home right now. But don't you have no uneasiness, Doctor, I've got him beat this time, and she'll not drag. No, sir, not till I do" — and a fierce spirit gleamed out through his eyes.

We had often wondered why Uncle Rube, the genial, gentle, hospitable old man that the

209

coast knew him to be, had come to put down his anchors in this wild and almost desolate gorge. Here was a possible explanation. The loss of his only lad must have been from this very Manxman, and by some strange twist of mentality the father had determined to plant himself just as near the scene and circumstance as human strength permitted, and there, single-handed if need be, fight out the battle of life, with the daily sense of flaunting the enemy that had robbed him of his joy in life — his one and only child. For with Chestertonian paradox this lonely man's passion was children.

"No. No, he can't move her, Doctor," he repeated, as if he were reading my thoughts, as I truly believe that he was. For our minds in the North are not crusted like tender feet with horny coverings from the chafe of boots, or as are minds beset with telephones, special deliveries, and editions of the yellow press.

"No, Uncle Rube, you don't think I'd sit here if I was n't certain of it. You've got him beaten to a frazzle this time."

The Red Island Shoals

I was right then, for Uncle Rube "slacked away" as he put it, and took up the thread of his story again without further comment, but not before apologizing for any undue familiarity into which the excitement, of which he was well aware, might have betrayed him.

"Us found t' seals early that year, and panned a voyage of as fine young fat as ever a 'swiler' wished for, but t' weather was dirty from t' day us struck t' patch, as if Jack Frost was determined us should n't have 'em. Anyhow, afore we could pick up more 'n half what us'd killed, a dozen o' our lads got adrift on t' floe, and though they got aboard another vessel, us thought 'em was lost. While us sailed about looking for 'em, us lost most o' t' pans. So round t' beginning of April t' skipper, in company with a score of other schooners, put her for the Norrard, in hopes of cutting off some of t' old seals in t' swatches. T' slob being very heavy outside, us lay for inside Belle Isle, and carried open water most across t' Straits. Well, sir, t' wind veered round all of a sudden, just as us was abeam of t' Devil's

Table, and t' Gulf ice came out of t' Straits
fair roaring" — and Uncle Rube took another
contemplative puff at his pipe.

"It would have been all right if only t' big
field had gone off t' same time before t' wind.
But somehow there were a big block held up
by t' Islands, and t' western ice just came and
hit it clip! It must have been all up with us
right there but for t' northeast current, and
that took our vessel like a nutshell and whisked
her away in t' heavy slob as if to carry her
along the Labrador coast. But it proved us
was not far enough off t' land, for just about
midday t' Red Islands come up like dark
specks out o' t' ice — right ahead t' way we
was being driven. T' other schooners was
caught in t' jam too and drifting with us,
little black dots scattered over t' surface of t'
ice field like t' currants in slices of sweet white
loaf.

"I believe our skipper knowed it were no
good, just as soon as t' watch called him to see
for hisself. But he made out as if there was
nothing to it, and ordered all hands to be

ready to take t' ice, as though 't was a patch o' swiles instead of rocks ahead. But when he started getting up grub, and canvas, and all sorts of things, and had us put 'em in t' boats, us knew it were no old harps he was thinking of.

"Well, sir, it seemed as if it had to be. The old Manxman went as fair for them reefs as if she was being hauled there with a capstan. It was fair uncanny, and I believes there be more in some one driving her there than most people 'lows. Anyhow, tied up as us was in t' heavy jam, right fair towards 'em she had to go, and then on to 'em, and up over t' reef as if us 'd laid t' course express for 'em, while every other vessel round us went clear. T' reef 's about five feet out o' water at high springs, and about ten feet over surface on t' neaps. Springs it was that day, t' moon being nearly full, and t' first crack ripped t' bottom clean out o' t' old ship. Us all hustled out on to t' ice, taking with us all us could carry, working as quick as ever us could, for t' pressure o' wind was rafting t' pans on to t' rocks, and almost before us knew it, what remained of her above t' ice had gone right on over t' shoals; and long before dusk, I reckons, had gone down through it. At any rate, us saw no more of her. Us tried to make a bit of shelter for t' night out o' some of t' canvas, but t' wind never slacked a peck, and t' rafting ice soon carried away even t' few things us had saved.

"Had us known in time us had better have stuck to t' boats, for they might have given us a chance. But t' wind being offshore, and t' ice running out to sea, made it seem safer to keep to t' rocks. For t' Red Island Shoal is only three or four miles from t' land, and there be liveyers, as us knew, almost opposite. If t' wind had held in t' same direction even then us might have escaped, but it dropped suddenly about day dawn, and there were huge swatches o' water between us and t' mainland before it came light enough to try and get across. Then just as suddenly t' wind clipped round, and t' sea began to make, and t' water started breaking right over them rocks.

"Us had managed to build a fire out o' some

The Red Island Shoals

of t' wreckage saved, and had thrown in bits o' canvas and some tarry oakum to make smoke. They had seen it too on t' land, and had lit three smoke fires in a line to let us know that they would send help if they could. But the veering of the wind had made that impossible, for they could only launch small skiffs, and they would not have lived more 'n a few minutes for t' ice making on 'em.

"T' breaking seas and driving spray soon wet all our men through. There were forty of us all told. But by night several were either dead or beyond help. T' ice had taken our boats, and now t' seas took all that was left. T' fire went out just before midday, and our bit o' grub got wet and frozen. Next morning t' sea was higher than ever, and t' bodies of t' men mostly washed away as they died. All that day t' rest of us just held on, some twenty or so; but it was a bare six of us that were living t' second night. There was no sleep, and not even any lying down if you wanted to live. None of them that slept ever woke again. I might have nodded standing up. Guess I must

215

have. But t' third morning I was t' only man moving; and though it was as fine a shining morning as ever broke, and t' hot sun from t' ice soon put a little life in me, I never expected to see another night. Then I must have forgotten everything, even t' people on t' shore. For I never saw any boat coming, or any one land. Everything had been washed away but myself. I had been alone, I reckon, many hours. It seemed ages since I'd heard a human voice; but I still remembers some one putting his hand on my shoulder. They had been calling, so they told me, but somehow I heard nothing. They kept me a good many days before I knowed anything — doing for me like a mother would for her boy. But more 'n a week had gone by before I could tell 'em who I was.

"And then it all came back to me — t' cruel suffering of my shipmates, and most of all of Willy, t' only chick or child I ever had. He had my coat over his oil frock, and he were so brave, so young, and so strong. And he lived till morning — long after great strong men had perished — and me able to do nothing.

The Red Island Shoals

Then his poor frozen body was washed to and fro in that terrible surf, as if my boy would n't leave me even if he was dead. Why I lived on, and why it pleased God to spare my poor life I never knowed, or shall know, Doctor, till he tells me himself."

He was sitting bolt upright now, looking me straight in the face. But the fire died suddenly from Uncle Rube's eyes, and, exhausted by the effort and the memories the story brought back to him, he fell back in the chair as if he had been struck by some knock-out blow. The thud of the fall once more woke the child, and, seeing me jump to the old man's help, she began to sob piteously. It was only for a moment, however. The splendid vitality of the man, toughened by his hard life and simple fare, soon made him master of himself again, and, apologizing for giving me trouble, he took up the child, crooning over her to get her quiet.

"Forty years I've been living here, Doctor," he went on. "Forty years — and t' last ten I've been all alone. Not a living soul have I had t' chance to save all these long years, though God knows I've kept as good a lookout as one watch could. Then Neighbor Blake lost his helpmate like I had mine, and he let me share up with him, and have Nellie. He wanted his boys to help him get food and things for t' rest, so a girl was what he gave me. And I could n't have had a boy, Doctor, anyhow. Willy's place will never be filled for me, till he comes himself and fills it, and that won't be long now either." He looked at his pipe, which had gone out, and then continued: "No, I'm not one o' them as can take a new wife almost as soon as t' first one's gone" — and then suddenly: "But it's time to boil t' kettle. You'se getting hungry, I 'lows, and me chattering like a fool, and not thinking of anything beyond my own troubles. I'm forgetting you must be worriting over being kept so long in this bit of a tilt, but you'll not get away till morning, so just make yourself as miserable as you can!"

As he bustled around filling the kettle with ice for water, and struggling to heat up a small molasses barrel in order to let out some "sweetness" for our tea, I had made a bird, a boat, and a couple of darts out of paper, as overtures to the lady of the house. Before the humble meal was spread she had the room ringing with her laughter, as she darted now here, now there, and at last succeeded in hitting the old man himself almost in the eye. Many times that meal has come back to my memory. The rough bare boards of the walls, naked but for one old picture of a horse cut from a magazine, carefully pasted upside down, and probably designed chiefly to cover some defective spot that was admitting too much coldness; the crazy table shaking with every gust and causing a tiny kerosene lamp to flare up and menace the dim religious darkness by depositing even more lamp-black than was its wont on its already negrine globe; the meagre board of dark bread, "oleo," and molasses; the weird minstrelsy of the hurricane — the whole a harmony of poverty and war. Yet the memory brings deeper pleasure to my mind than that of many costly banquets

— and even I have eaten from plates of silver with implements of gold. For in the flickering light of the crackling logs I can still see the joy of the old man's kindly face over the boisterous happiness of his quaint ward, the dance in the eyes of the merry child as some colored candies placed in my nonny-bag by my wife fell somehow from the sky right on to the table before her. The telling of his story, never before mentioned to any one but his wife and foster child, but kept like some vendetta wrong waiting for revenge in his rebellious heart these many years, seemed to have renewed his youth. A merrier, happier party it has never been my lot to share in; and now that I know the pathos of the last chapter written in this strange life, I rejoice more than ever that for that night, anyhow, the enemy that haunted him overreached, and the very blizzard proved the key for one evening at least of freedom from his obsession.

We were away before daylight, and I never saw Uncle Rube again. Life, it seems, went along tranquilly with him the following winter.

The Red Island Shoals

As usual he kept his watch and ward on the cliffs by the Red Island Shoals. Then the fatal 10th of April came round. Once again it broke upon the solitary figure of the old man straining his eyes from his coign of vantage on the dread shoals of the Red Islands. Unquestionably he saw again reënacted there the weird tragedy that nearly half a century before had broken his life, bringing home with a strange fascination the moving picture to his very heart. But with it this spring he witnessed also a scene that for many years every man on the coast had prayed for, but no man had been privileged to take part in. The wind had come out of the Straits and the Gulf ice was driving swiftly towards the great Atlantic, exactly as it had done on the memorable day now forty years before. Once again there was ice in huge sheets jammed against the great cliffs of Belle Isle, and clear water between. Suddenly the straining eyes of the old sailor shone with a totally new light. He jumped to his feet, and with hands shading his starting eyes, stood motionless like a statue on the pedestal of his lookout, now white as the purest marble in its winter mantle.

Was it age? Or the final break-up of his mind? No, neither — he was certain of it. There were black things moving on the white ice, and driving with it once more, just as the Manxman had, straight for the shoals of the Red Islands. Nearer and nearer they came. There could be no doubt now. They moved. They could be no land débris, no shadows from the rafted ice sheets. So quickly was the floe running that just as he remembered it, before anything could be done, clip! and the advancing edge had again struck the standing ice, and woe betide anything that was in or on it, anywhere near the line of contact. As a dazed mouse watches the cat that is toying with it, the rigid figure on the hilltop gazed at the impending tragedy — too far off for his material brain correctly to interpret the image on his actual retina. He was seeing, though he failed to realize it, the same impress that emotion had recorded on the tablets of his very soul.

The realism of it was too much for human

The Red Island Shoals

nature, and Uncle Rube, his hands covering his face, started running homewards over the familiar pathway he had trodden so often. Even as he reached the cottage in the gulch he was aware of loud shouting, and of a team of huskies literally tearing over the snow. They were making as if to pass his house without stopping, as no man ever did that lonely spot, if only for the cup of tea and the moment's "spell," and the kindly stimulus of the old man's company. Yes, the driver was shouting, shouting to him. "Ships, Uncle Rube!" — "What is it?" — "Ships on the ice!" the old man heard. Did n't he know it only too well?

Another moment and the modern Paul Revere, with dogs for horses and ice and snow for a highway, was flying on his self-imposed journey, carrying his slogan from house to house and village to village along the sparsely inhabited coast-line. As Uncle Rube opened his door and peered into the little room, to his infinite joy he saw the golden curls in their proper place on the old settle by the stove, while the regular quiet breathing assured him that the child had not yet waked from sleep. As he softly tiptoed around, seeking the outfit he needed for his great adventure, the barrenness of the house, the poverty of it, struck him for the first time. God knows he had never thought of "things," except as he had needed them for himself or others; and now he wished suddenly that he had more of them for the child's sake. Suppose, now that his "day" had at last arrived, he should not return from the long-looked-for quest. He became strangely conscious that he had nothing laid up for his darling, the child who now filled the whole horizon of his cramped life. Her very clothes were in tatters. The Indian shawl, that I had seen pressed into the service against his enemy the Frost King, was now only a thing of rags and patches. Were it not for his own big coat, even at this moment his Princess would be shivering with cold. Furtively he glanced round for his rope and gaff, relics of the last time he had gone on the ice. All these years he had kept them ready for "the day," never able to break the spell woven around them on the

The Red Island Shoals

ill-fated Manxman. There was his nonny-bag, in it already the sugar and oatmeal, the ration of pork, and the small bottle of brandy, that each year he kept ready when the 10th of March came round — the day on which the sealers leave for the ice fields. The new idea that his life was of value for the child's sake sent a half-guilty feeling through him, lest he be caught looking at these implements, where they lay with his old converted flintlock gun on the rack above the still glowing stove. Sh! The child on the settle muttered something in her sleep, and the old man, rigid as an ice block, stood listening to her breathing, as if he were a burglar robbing a rich man's bedroom, in which the owner himself lay sleeping. But she quieted down again, and once more he breathed freely.

At last he was ready, all but the big coat. Well, he could do without that. If he were not back before dark the difference it would make would anyhow be negligible. There was no time to delay. He must go now or never; and the indomitable old warrior stooped over to kiss the child good-bye, though he dare only touch with his lips the golden hair, for fear of waking her. Then in his simple way he breathed a wordless prayer, committing her to God's keeping, and, stealthily letting himself out, made straight for the likeliest part of the headland from which to take the ice.

As one thinks now of that old man setting out alone over that endless ocean of ice, one wonders if one has one's self ever attempted anything heroic. But Uncle Rube thought only of one thing that morning — of foiling his arch enemy on the Red Island Shoals; and though nearly fourscore years had passed over him, he felt like a lad of twenty as he strode rapidly along towards the landwash.

Of course he must haul his boat, but that he could easily do. Had he not built her himself expressly, small, and of half-inch planking over the lightest of frames, with two bilge streaks to act as runners, and flat-bottomed that she should drag well over snow? When at length he had launched her over the "ballicater" ice, and had pulled her clear of the cracks by the

The Red Island Shoals

landwash, he stopped and spent a grudgingly spared moment in lighting his pipe. Then, heigho, and away for the open sea — out on to which he marched with his head erect and his old heart dauntless, like the peaceful Minute-Men of 1776.

Meanwhile an ever-increasing crowd of men, women, and even children were pouring from apparently nowhere out on to the floe. The young men were "copying," as we say, over the ice, that is, jumping from pan to pan as they ventured far out from the land seeking the seals which the running ice, driving out before the wind, had brought down from the Gulf, and then killing them, and hauling them back into safety.

It was from them that I subsequently learned the story of the day. Before night fell the wind had risen, and blew directly from the land. Snow began to fall soon after mid-day, and by sundown a living blizzard howled over the frozen ocean. None of the distant neighbors had seen Uncle Rube set out; none of them even knew that he had left his house;

no one before ever heard of his doing such a thing as start out on the ice alone. Nor was it till the next day that a half-frozen little girl, who was heard crying in the snow in front of a neighbor's house, disclosed the secret that Uncle Rube was missing.

How had they known at all that there were seals on the ice that day? Known? Why, Mark Seaforth had gone all along the coast telling them early in the morning. He had got the news from the lighthouse, and it was the oldest of customs to give all hands a chance whenever the seals were sighted driving alongshore.

It had not been the material ear drum to which the old man had listened for his sailing orders. On that day especially he had heard with other ears, and all the coast freed Mark from any blame for the old sailor's having understood "ships" instead of "seals."

Late in the sealing season of that same year the good ship Artemis, a stout, steel-sheathed ice hunter, a unit of the modern fleet that have long ago displaced the wooden schooners that once in hundreds followed the seal herds, was

The Red Island Shoals

steaming north to finish up shooting old harps in the swatches, having lost a number of her pans in bad weather farther south. Seals were scarce on the west side, and the wireless had warned the skipper that a patch of old seals was passing eastward through the Straits. Cape Bauld Light had been sighted, and so also had the new light on Belle Isle. The bar-relmen were eagerly scanning the ice for any signs of the expected herd.

"Something black on the ice on the port bow!" shouted the man from the foretop.

"Where away?" answered the master of the bridge.

"About four points to the northwest."

"Hard astarboard!" from the bridge.

"Starboard hard!" from the wheel, and the big ship wheeled a course direct for the Red Island Shoals.

"Steady!" from the bridge.

"Steady it is!" And the Artemis wheeled a little more, and leaving the shoals on her right, steamed towards the object that had attracted the attention of the watch. The bridge master, viewing it through his glasses, suddenly stopped short, fixing his gaze on the spot with far more than his wonted intensity.

"What is it, John?" he said to the watchman. "Seems queer to me. It's no seal, I'll swear."

John took the glasses, and, putting them to his eyes, made out at once what the object was.

"'T is a small boat upside down — and yes, there's a man's body for certain, stretched out beside it," he announced in a subdued voice.

"Go slow!" to the engine man.

"Slow!" rang back the watchful engineer.

"Stop her!" and over the side went half a dozen men.

"Take that hatch over, and bring in the man off the ice."

All the crew, some three hundred blackened figures, were now leaning over the rail to see the evidence of this latest tragedy. No one knew him, or could even guess where he and his boat had come from, or on what strange quest he had been bound. Those ice pans might have come from anywhere along the hundreds

The Red Island Shoals

of miles between Anticosti and Cape Chidley. To these men, it was just the body of an old man, a stranger. Not much loss. He could not have lived many more years, anyhow. Probably no one would miss him. No need to trouble over it. A prompt burial at sea, thought the captain, would be as good as on the land, where a grave was an impossibility now, anyhow. Besides, he was obviously an old seaman, and what could be more appropriate? Moreover, the crew would rather have it so than to carry the corpse around while they were seal-hunting.

There was no parson aboard, but the skipper was a God-fearing man. So the flags were hauled to half-mast, the ship hove to the wind, the crew called on deck just as they were, and when the skipper had read a brief prayer, "in sure and certain hope" the body of Uncle Reuben Marston, vanquished by his enemy at last, was committed to the deep within a biscuit toss of the Red Island Shoals.

THE END

* 9 7 8 1 5 8 9 6 3 8 5 8 7 *